I0535143

DOUBLE DOOM

SHADOWS OVER ELISTA, BOOK 4

CLARA WILS

Gryphon's Gate Publishing

Double Doom

Gryphon's Gate Publishing
550 King St. N.
PO Box 42088 Conestoga
Waterloo, ON
N2L 6K5

Print ISBN: 978-1-990587-17-7

CHAPTER 1

SWIFT

I groaned. My body hurt... everywhere.

I blinked my eyes open, light stabbing into my brain, adding to my pains. The sun had just risen above the trees. I groaned again, it seemed to help me move, as I rolled to my side then slowly to my hands and knees, head hanging.

What had happened? My head was fuzzy, aching, like the rest of me. I felt like I'd been stepped on by some giant, not enough to crush me, but enough to bruise me all over.

Swan attacked you, Isoa said, concerned. *She used some strange magic to swat you away from her, then...* Isoa shuddered within me. *I've never felt pain like that before, nor such odd powers. That woman terrifies me.*

I had to agree. The memories returned with Isoa's

words. I'd been escorting Dawn and Roo, then... that woman!

I surged to my feet despite my pain, but it quickly became clear to me, some time had passed. We'd been fleeing at night, and it was early morning now. Swan was gone, everyone was gone, except...

Falcon!

I ran to my brother. We'd both been thrown some distance from where we had tried to attack Swan. He was also just starting to rouse, but he'd been further to the east of me, and was still in the shadow of tall trees, the sun hadn't reached him yet to help wake him, as it had with me.

"Falcon!" I shouted as I fell to my knees next to him.

He groaned, eyes blinking open. "Am I alive? I must be alive; if I were dead, I don't think I'd hurt this much." His eyes focused on me. "Brother? What... happ—?" His eyes went wide as he must have remembered. "Are Dawn and Roo well?"

"I don't know. I just woke myself. They're not here. It's the next day."

"Then they were taken or killed," he said, lips curling sourly. I wasn't sure why he thought that, but he then explained. "If they had survived the attack, they would be the ones rousing us, and it would probably still be night. Something bad has happened." He sat up slowly. "Is Pan still here?"

"I haven't looked. I found you first." I stood, surveying the area, but the low stumps of long burned-out trees and the new scrub-brush made it hard to see much. We were also on the far side of the river from where the others had been. I veered and took to the skies. I saw Pan soon after that. Swooping down to the small man, I landed, changed back, and shouted for Falcon to join me. Then I knelt next to Pan.

By the Spirits! Isoa gasped. I had to agree. Pan was covered in blood from some wound on his chest. His usually pale skin was deathly grey. He had to be dead.

But when I touched his cheek he started and groaned, though he didn't regain consciousness.

"Spirits! You're still alive after this?" I whispered. Then I put pressure on the wound as we'd been taught to do.

When Falcon landed, I told him to tear off his shirt and give it to me, I stuffed that over the wound, pressing hard. Falcon then took over for me as I removed my shirt and we used the long arms of that to tie around the small man's narrow chest and press our make-shift bandage in place.

Ceph, Isoa said, bringing a bit of clarity into my pain and grief addled mind. I nodded.

"We need to get him to Ceph now," I said. "Your falcon's eyes are keener than my swift's. Go, look for the others, bring them here." We swapped out again, and I returned to tending Pan. Dawn would kill me if I let him die.

"It would be a true blessing of the Spirits if they're still alive," Falcon said softly before taking off.

I had to agree. Last night had been truly horrid. The only true battles I'd fought before this had been in the north and we'd been prepared, had strategies, and won, even against a force with superior numbers. But... this had been our first time fighting a true dragon lord and his armies.

And we'd failed.

Swan had crushed us. The previous time we'd engaged her, I'd not challenged her directly. I'd fought her minions and fared well. But this time... Swan had swatted us away like flies, like we were nothing. How was one supposed to fight something like that?

I do not know, I wish I could help more, but... I've never seen anything like Swan before. Isoa was still rattled, I could tell. They weren't helping my sour mood.

I gritted my teeth in frustration as I kept pressure on Pan's wound.

It seemed even Pan hadn't fared well last night, though I didn't know the specifics of how he'd come by this wound. And... if Dawn and Roo together — perhaps two of the strongest True-Bonded to come out of Silverveil — couldn't defeat Swan, then...

Falcon landed. "Nothing in my first pass around. It's... a mess out there. There are thousands of dead in the forest, mostly the dragon lord's men. I'll keep looking." And he was off again.

Well, that was one piece of good news at least. Even with the army we'd gathered we'd been hopelessly outnumbered. We'd sent a force of not quite a thousand men out to slow that army, while a few hundred remained with the long column of nearly two thousand refugees. I hoped they had gotten away safely, but at this point, I had little hope for them. I'd seen how easily Swan had incinerated the refugees near us. One beam of that red-energy of hers and she'd killed two dozen people easily.

How are we supposed to fight that?

We'll find a way, Isoa said, but they didn't sound hopeful at all.

It seemed to take forever for Falcon to return again, yet the sun had barely shifted in the sky when I heard his wings and felt — through our joined spirit-bond — him returning.

A small octopus was dropped on the ground next to me, along with a rhinoceros beetle.

All three men shifted to their human forms. Ceph looked haggard and worn, but he pushed me aside and went to work on Pan. Rhino sat heavily, looking a bit dazed and confused. He didn't say anything, but I could almost feel the defeat and self-loathing radiating from him as he eventually laid down and just kept shaking his head.

"See if you can find Lyran," Ceph said, voice raspy and hoarse. I wasn't sure if he was addressing me or Falcon, but then... we could both be out searching now. We looked at each other, nodded, then veered, heading into the skies in different directions.

The most notable thing from this height, was the burned-out forest to the north. I didn't know what had stopped that fire, perhaps the winds had turned, but it looked like it had destroyed a large chunk of forest.

And though it was hard to see through the thick canopy of the forest below, I marveled at what I did see. Falcon had been right, there were so many dead down there, most of them in the red and black of the dragon lord's army. Whatever else had happened last night, our forces had fought bravely and well.

I circled higher. Over the immediate area of the battle, I could see no sign of Lyran and Eophon, and one would think a dragon would be easy to see.

I began to wonder if they had fled. I didn't think it possible, but it would explain the lack of a massive dragon. Or perhaps Lyran's fight with his brother had not gone well at all, and he'd been incinerated? Was that a thing that could happen with dragons? I didn't know enough of their kind.

I soared out to the east and south, leaving the area of the battle behind. It was also possible that dragon-combat in the skies might have taken them far away from the battle below.

There! To the south! Isoa called, and I felt where they were indicating.

I saw a straight-line swath of the forest which had been cleared. Curious, I flew closer, and I saw Eophon, looking dead, splayed and broken at the end of that long line of crushed trees.

Oh Blessed Spirits, no, Isoa gasped.

I rushed to the scene to see if Lyran was nearby. On my first pass around the area, I didn't see any man-shaped objects. I travelled back up the swath of broken trees and there, barely visible through the shattered branches and brush, was Lyran, body at an odd angle amidst low thick branches and broken trees. I swooped lower and landed next to him.

Blessed Spirits, I cursed. His body was broken, arms and legs bending in the wrong directions with bones poking out from broken skin. And his face... was unrecognizable, crushed.

Yet, amazingly his chest was still moving, a soft, high wheeze escaping that mess of a face.

I needed to bring Ceph here immediately.

I took off and began shrieking, calling out to Falcon, trying to let him know I'd found Lyran and Eophon.

The falcon nearby flew closer and circled the crash site as I sped back to Ceph.

When I returned, Pan was sitting, blinking, looking a bit stunned to be alive.

I veered back to human before I landed, dropping a few feet to the ground. "I found Lyran, he's in a bad way, but still alive. He needs you."

Ceph looked exhausted — heavy bags under life-less eyes, face slack, shoulder's drooping — but he nodded, rising.

"I can help," Pan said, voice sounding a bit hoarse. "I can borrow your gift, heal myself then help with Lyran."

Ceph looked at him and shrugged. The man was truly drained and soul-weary, I could tell that much. Pan touched Ceph to regain the man's spirit-gift.

"I can't carry you," I said to Pan. "Even your avatar form is too big, too heavy."

Pan rose tentatively. "Take Ceph. I'll alter myself, make myself smaller and lighter, so Falcon can carry me. He can lift a bit more weight than you, yes?"

I nodded.

As I veered into my swift form, Ceph shrank into a small octopus, and I picked up his awkward form. He must have been doing something to make himself lighter as well, as he seemed to weigh nothing.

I hurried to where Lyran lay, hoping Ceph would have enough left in him to bring Lyran back from the brink of death.

CHAPTER 2

CEPH

I HADN'T SLEPT. I'D FOUGHT FOR MY LIFE AS LONG AS there had been enemies around me, and when I had found no more, I'd been wounded and weary. I'd healed myself, then gone in search of other survivors. I'd encountered other patches of fighting, helping where I could, fighting and healing in equal measure.

Then… I'd found Rhino.

I didn't know what had happened to him, His face had been crushed as had his breastplate. I'd thought he was dead, until I touched him and felt a faint beat of life. So, I'd healed him, weakening his overall body greatly to stitch back together his face and mend the broken ribs in his chest. Then I'd collapsed. Perhaps I had slept then, as it was suddenly morning and Falcon was approaching. Yet, if I had slept, somehow I'd felt even worse than I had the night before, exhausted and soul weary.

And Falcon's news: that Dawn and Roo had been taken... hadn't done much to help my flagging spirit. Yet once Rhino had woken and heard the news, he was up quickly... though his legs were so weak he could barely stand. We'd transformed, and Falcon had taken us to Pan.

Another man near to death. A stroke to the heart, but... oddly the wound was mostly superficial. Pan had a tough hide on him, and the blade had pierced his heart, but only just. The blood had even semi-coagulated keeping more from leaving him. Still, he'd been a hair's-breadth away from death. I'd mended the tiny puncture to the heart and sealed the wound over it, but not much more. That had been enough for him to wake, weak as he was.

Even if he borrowed my gift, he had little energy to heal himself or others. I hadn't wanted to discourage him, though. The six of us were a family now, brothers, and each as dedicated to our women as any one man was to his wife.

Swift set me down next to Lyran at the base of a tree. I veered back to human form and felt a lone tear escape my eye, partially from seeing Lyran's broken form and partially because I was already so far gone to fatigue I didn't know if I could heal him.

Next to me, Swift returned to human form, balancing on a branch above me. "Eophon is also nearby and looks just as bad."

Some part of my spirit broke in that moment; I'd have to heal a near-to-dead dragon too? It was impossible. I think I flinched or whimpered because Swift then asked: "Are you well?"

No, I wasn't. This was all too much. Still, I tried to smile up at Swift. "I'll do what I can."

Swift nodded at that.

Only then did I notice how weary and haggard he looked as well. We had all had a rough night.

I'll give you what strength I can, Ulio said solemnly.

For once I was thankful for the usually annoying Lumani. He'd said exactly what I needed to hear. *Thank you.*

I moved next to Lyran. He was alive; I could hear his wheeze of a breath. But, by all the Spirits, I had no clue how he had survived. I'd thought that a lot recently: about Rhino and Pan both. Turned out, we were a tough bunch, hard to kill.

I put my hands to his chest, his clothes had been torn away by something, his torso crisscrossed with shallow cuts. I felt into him, seeking the damage done to his body, the worst of it to fix. I also sought the healthy part, from which I could take undamaged tissue to move to the broken areas. The trouble was, unlike the others, there wasn't much of Lyran that wasn't broken. Which meant I had to be specific and careful as I tried to mend him, not easy when I was already so tired.

I concentrated on his face first, another unrecognizable mess, like Rhino's had been. The body remembered the shape and structure and I let it mend itself as I moved traces of healthy tissue and bone to that area. That alone seemed to take forever. When I looked up, resting myself for just a moment before continuing on, Swift was gone. I went back to work, knowing I'd not be able to mend every broken bone right now, I focused on simply closing the wounds where the most blood was being lost. I sealed up the body as best I could. The hope was that eventually, when I was rested and so was Lyran, I'd be able to return for another session, without him having died in the meantime.

And when I was done, I collapsed. I wanted to walk, wanted to find Eophon and do what I could, but I knew there would be nothing I could do now. I needed sleep. So, I stayed where I'd fallen and curled into a ball to rest. I only hoped Lyran could forgive me the loss of his dragon. There was nothing I could do for the majestic beast. And in my soul, I wept for that loss.

My eyes closed, but images of death and battle haunted my dreams.

"Eophon."

The word, an anguished and broken sound, woke me from an uneasy slumber. I rolled over, looking at Lyran, who had somehow managed to rise. I was amazed he could stand. His body was still broken in so many ways, but his spirit must be compelling him. He leaned heavily against a tree; one arm outstretched.

"Eophon," he uttered again. Then he tried to take a step.

"Lyran, no!" I called, surging to my feet, but it was too late. Lyran's shattered body couldn't support his weight and as soon as he moved away from that tree, he fell. The area around us was a mess of fallen branches, jagged-edged and dangerous. Lyran slammed down on a particularly sharp one, which punched through his chest and out his back.

"Lyran!" I shouted, scrambling over to him. Pulling him off the branch, I rolled him over. Instantly, through my gift, I felt the *wrongness* within him. He was bleeding profusely and dying all the swifter.

"Pits," I swore.

Ulio, if you have anything left—

I know, it's yours. Save him if you can.

I wept, jaw clenched, and went to work on Lyran again. If I didn't, he'd be dead within minutes.

But... the problem remained of so little of him which was healthy enough to move to other areas. I... just couldn't.

But... tired as I was, I was mostly healthy... so I took from myself, instead. It was... sickening, feeling all the horrid shattering of another's broken body taken upon myself as I swapped out healthy for broken. I wasn't breaking myself per se, but I was taking on wounded cells and tissue, weakening myself dramatically and it quickly became apparent, if I kept doing this, I'd simply pass out, I'd not be physically strong enough to keep healing Lyran.

So, I stopped taking physically from myself and tore at my own spirit-gift, seeking more strength, more ability, more power

Ceph, no, you can't do this, you'll burn yourself out! Ulio cried within me.

I have to or he dies, and Roo would never forgive me for that. What is the cost of my gift when compared with another's life?

But your gift could heal so many more than just one man.

But it's this one man who counts the most for me and those I love. I'm sorry, Ulio.

As am I.

I ripped at my spirit, breaking the gift which had been given to me, pouring more healing into Lyran. His bones mended, his body healed, and I knew he would live.

But I also knew... I would never be able to use my gift again. All that remained of my spirit-gift was shreds and tatters. I felt... hollow, used up, more than just sickened but frail, diminished, broken.

I would have thrown up anything in my stomach, if I hadn't already used up everything inside me. I retched and wept and twitched with utter desolation.

But at least I knew... Lyran would live.

CHAPTER 3

PAN

Falcon dropped me at Eophon and I returned to my Fey form, laying a hand on the dragon.

I had switched my power, borrowing Ceph's gift when I'd awoken, knowing I'd need it to heal myself further. But now... that was gone from my mind. My hurt was nothing compared to the immensity of damage done to this huge living being.

And Eophon wasn't dead, despite their wounds. I guessed it took a lot to kill a dragon. Yet, they did seem to be in some form of deep hibernation or sleep, body functions slowed and stilled. That had been what had kept them alive this long, but they were still dying... just slower.

"By The Lights and Shadows!" I whispered.

"Can you save them?" Falcon asked.

"I have no clue, but I'll try."

I don't know much of healing. I was a warrior in my previous life. But I'll give you what strength I can, Eona whispered within me. Her voice was low and reverent with awe, being this close to a dragon.

I'll take what I can get, thanks.

I felt within Eophon, seeking what was broken, to begin the process of replacing damaged parts with healthy tissue. But it quickly became clear that far more was broken than was not. There was the massive gash along their belly and another on their right flank, plus all four legs were broken, several bones through the long spinal column between neck and the end of the long tail were also broken, not to mention one wing was nearly torn off and the other was crushed and crumpled. As the dragon had crashed, branches hadn't done much to the tough hide, but full trees had, leaving heavy bruises and a few deep gouges as well. There was still a lot of undamaged tissue within the great form, but not enough. So, I focused on the most serious wounds first, the great gashes and gouges, and the more serious of the broken bones, but even before these were healed, I sensed another problem... my own limits of power and endurance.

I was already weak. I'd lost a lot of blood from the wound in my chest. Ceph had said it hadn't been that deep, thankfully, but it had still cost me much, and I had been nowhere near full strength when I'd started healing Eophon.

I stepped away, collapsing to my knees, breathing hard, drenched in sweat.

"Is... are you well?" Falcon asked. Rhino was here now, as was Swift.

I shook my head. "I'm weak, and there are too many injuries."

"Can you take strength from us?" Falcon asked.

"I... don't know." I was only borrowing this power. I hadn't had it for as long as Ceph had.

Falcon swore. He seemed to consider things for a long moment, then asked: "With what you've done so far, will Eophon live at least?"

"I don't know." The wounds were still extensive. With Eophon's dormant state, even if he was still dying, I'd given him more time, but I didn't know how much: hours or days?

"Is there anything else you can do?" Falcon asked, clearly at his wit's end.

I'd been about to say no, when Eona piped up.

What about your Fey abilities?

My... I can manipulate iron, metal. How would that help? But it was something. I didn't think about my Fey abilities much these days. Yet...

"I... may have more... I can do?" An idea was starting to form in my mind. As much as I hadn't used my Fey abilities in some time, I'd been well trained and apprenticed, before I'd run off with Dawn to see the world. If I could... somehow... manipulate metal and a being's physiology at the same time... then...?

I had no clue what might be possible.

We can try and see what happens, Eona suggested.

Given my natural sensitivity to metal, I knew — just from having possessed Ceph's ability a little — that bodies possessed metal. It wasn't in a truly usable form, but it was there, sort of. And... if I could take metals from the earth around me...

Metals and...

The Fey who had the ability to work with metals could also manipulate some other elements, like carbon, to make stronger metals, such as incredibly light and strong steel.

Yes, I know you can do it! Eona cheered me on.

Here goes... something, I said as I shuffled over to Eophon kneeling next to the massive body. I put one hand on it, the other on the ground. I felt down, deep into the earth. It wasn't something I was used to doing, especially since Ceph's ability was new to me, but I tried a combination of my two powers, seeking carbon specifically from the earth. It would be that element which I'd need most to remake Eophon.

Carbon was everywhere, in almost everything, but it wasn't what I was used to working with, especially since I was using my metal powers as a link to use Ceph's powers with non-biological sources. I didn't even fully understand it, but I... felt in my bones it would work. Oh! Bones! Calcium, I'd need that too.

Tired as I was, I felt the sources of what I needed, all around me, I sensed their presence in the earth and plants and other living beings. Perhaps that's all Ceph's ability was, a sensitivity to the elements that made up a person and the power to shift them around. Knowing that, seemed to make it a little easier and I began to funnel the elements I needed out of the earth and the grasses and everything around me — that wasn't myself or one of the other guys — and push that into Eophon.

I became a conduit for the movement of materials and began to use that to mend Eophon's many ills. Bones began to knit, scales were remade, lighter and stronger, organs and innards were mended and reinforced. And I quickly realized. I wasn't just remaking Eophon, I was... upgrading them. Their copper-colored scales were already harder than steel, but now they'd be lighter and harder still. Their claws and fangs would be near to unbreakable, as would their bones. Their wings, perhaps one of the most vulnerable parts, would be like the finest, thinnest steel, strong and resilient but still light enough for them to fly.

Eophon woke, roaring and shifting. I leaped out of the way, or I would have been crushed.

But I wasn't finished my work.

"Still them!" I shouted to the others. "Let them know I'm healing them! Please!"

Swift, Falcon, and Rhino all moved around the dragon, trying to get their attention, shouting at them.

Eophon adjusted, since they had been laying on a shattered wing, which was now half-healed. They freed the wing, then roared — in what I assumed was pain — as they tried to stretch it out and use it. It was still broken.

What are you doing? The voice roared into my head and nearly overwhelmed me.

I didn't know if I could speak in my head back, so I shouted. "I'm mending you, making you stronger. Please let me help you!"

The massive beast groaned and sat down slowly. *There is... so much pain, but... I am alive. I had not thought that possible. Please continue, I am sorry for interrupting.*

Understandable.

I moved in again, connecting with Eophon and the ground, only then noticing the massive spot of blackened earth and dead plants emanating out from where I'd been. It was a great loss; Fey revered nature. Yet in this case, it would be well worth it to revitalize this amazing being.

I continued my work, feeling somehow refreshed. Apparently, pulling all of these elements from the earth was revitalizing myself as well, healing me of my weakness, filling me with the minerals I needed to live.

I didn't know if they were making me stronger in the same way as they were for Eophon, since I was just a conduit, but it might be an interesting side effect.

I do not know how long I worked, only that when I was finally done, exhausted, but more than satisfied with my work, the sun was in the west, falling behind trees... and I was famished.

Luckily the others had gone hunting and gathered berries and other food from the forest. I didn't eat meat, so the small game Falcon had caught had no interest for me, but the rest was fair game, and the others let me gorge myself to renew my spent energies.

I feel... different, Eophon said. And I knew everyone had heard it because we all looked over at the dragon.

"I remade you," I said, calling out to them. "I used all the minerals of the earth to rebuild you, better, tougher, faster, stronger, and lighter."

This is an amazing gift, thank you, little one.

"You're very welcome."

Eophon had turned their long neck around to look at the four of us and their gaze shifted, to where Ceph and Lyran lay. Rhino had gathered the two of them while I'd worked. Ceph was still unconscious, but Lyran was awake, if still healing and weak. Swift was helping the tall man take bits of food and water.

I am glad you survived, friend, Eophon said, I knew the words were meant for Lyran. *But I sense you are different too?*

Lyran nodded. "This one," he said indicating Ceph. "He... healed me from near death twice, if I understand him. He gave so much of himself that he is a part of me now. And... he also spent himself." To us, Lyran said. "His power is gone, burned out, used to save me."

It took a moment to hit me: Ceph's power was gone?

That meant...

I was the only one left in the party who could heal anyone.

I couldn't borrow any other powers from now on. If I did, I'd never be able to regain Ceph's power, it would be lost to all of us, and we needed it desperately. Without it, several of us wouldn't be here now.

I sat back heavily.

Somehow, I had become what Ceph had been. And Ceph... had nothing.

That didn't seem right.

But it was what it was.

I know you'll tend to this gift well, Eona said solemnly. *And when the time is right, we'll find a way to return it to Ceph.*

I hoped that was possible.

"We need to rest and regain our strength," Falcon said. "Dawn and Roo have been captured and as much as I know we all want to go after them now, if we did, we'd probably be captured too. We need to rest. And while we do, we can plan, and begin moving south, but..." He looked at Ceph, unconscious and looking so very frail, and Lyran who looked little better. "There isn't much we can do now."

And that sat heavily upon us all. I didn't truly know what the other's felt, but for me, needing to wait, knowing Dawn was out there and potentially hurt and in desperate need of me, was the worst possible feeling in existence.

CHAPTER 4

DAWN

T

HE RIDING CROP SLAMMED INTO MY STOMACH AGAIN. I would have doubled over in pain at the repeated punishment on the same spot, but I couldn't. My hands were manacled above my head, attached to chains anchored in the stone ceiling of my cell. I hung, toes only barely touching the ground, arms aching from the strain of holding my weight, as Swan tortured me.

And Swan was loving every moment of it, alternating between giddy giggling and shivering with what seemed a near orgasmic pleasure with each hit.

"Take this, you bitch!" Another hit to my stomach. I clenched my teeth so I wouldn't cry out, though tears escaped my eyes. The skin wasn't even torn, but it was red, raised and incredibly sensitive and painful already. She was very careful, very accurate with her strikes, only hitting that same, already swollen spot, just to aggravate it more and more. And since pressing on a wound only made it hurt more, she was being very effective in her pain delivery.

The spot on my stomach wasn't the only place she was focusing on. She'd spent some time slamming her riding crop against my left thigh, right buttocks, one of my breasts — that one had been the worst — and also my face, on my right cheek.

That last one I'd brought upon myself. With my feet free, I'd tried to kick out at her. But she had some sort of protective field around her and I'd not even hit her. She'd retaliated viciously, though. She'd said she wanted to keep my face perfect for now, but she'd easily forgotten that, breaking open my cheek, which throbbed with pain.

"This is what you get for killing my queen and my love, you stupid whore!" Another hard clap of the crop against my stomach and this time I did cry out.

She giggled.

I'd long ago realized she didn't care about me. I was just a convenient surrogate for all of this pent-up viciousness and anger was toward my mother.

She's also completely insane, Amya noted. The Lumani had been trying to help me, lending me strength, even though Amya couldn't truly heal me.

I know, and right now I don't want to aggravate her. I... may have an idea though... It was still forming, but perhaps I could appeal to some part of her insanity.

"I want you to die painfully, Legs!" This time a hit to my thigh, just to change things up, and the surprise re-introduction of pain to that already sore spot brought out another scream. "But first, before you die, I'm going to take everything you love from you!"

"I know," I said, experimenting.

The riding crop paused mid-swing.

I went on. "I submit to you, Swan. You win. I know you'll kill me, but... can I know one thing first?"

Those crazed eyes lifted to meet my gaze. "I know you're not actually Legs," she whispered. "I'm not mad. I'm not. I'm perfectly normal. You're crazy, not me." Her ramblings weren't a good sign for her sanity.

"I know," I said, and she smiled. It was working. I could appeal to her desperate superiority. And perhaps, I could even get some information from her at the same time.

"Good." She was practically purring.

"But..." And I put all my force of spirit into sounding defeated and pathetic. "How are you so powerful?"

Her smile grew and she preened, strutting around the small cell. "I *am* powerful." She slapped her own leg with the riding crop. "No pain. I am stronger than you."

"But... how?" I asked again.

She spun on me slapping a new spot on my side. "It's your fault, you bitch." A bit of clarity came to her eyes, and she amended herself. "It's your mother's fault... that I'm so powerful. She brought about her own destruction." That was interesting, if not entirely informative.

Swan continued her swaggering walk around behind me. "Do you like your mother?" she asked. That seemed an odd question to ask, but I wanted to keep her talking, so I played along.

"She's a queen and had little time for me. I felt abandoned. I hated her." I had already been weeping, but this admission of a partial — and very close to my heart — truth wrung more tears from me. Still, I needed to know more from Swan. "It's clear you don't like her much. What did she do to make you so powerful?"

"She killed my lover and my queen. I had power. I was still a new member of the Royal House, but after the old queen died and Merlin came to power, she saw my worth and elevated me. And that brought me into the arms of Hale. I loved him and he loved me. It was an eternal bond, and your bitch of a mother took all of that away from me!" A slap with her crop to the back of my leg. I could tell she was losing control, erratic now. She wasn't focusing on my pain-points, hitting me wherever she liked.

"And that made you powerful?"

A harsh laugh. "Indeed. I ran. For a long time, I ran, and my hate for her only grew and... then it blossomed into something amazing. I had always wanted a spirit-gift, and she gave me one. The incredible force of my need to see her suffer endowed me with the spirit-gift of revenge."

Revenge? Have you ever heard of anything like that, I asked Amya.

No, this is new, and for something so corrupted to take hold of her, her Lumani must be as insane as she is, as driven to cause pain and suffering. They're both mad.

Great.

"And a truly great power it is," I said, playing to her need for control once more. "You have that incinerating beam, a shield to protect you, you can throw things with your mind, and that scream you did on the road in Elista. No spirit-gift I've ever heard of is as powerful as that." I hoped this praise would get her to tell me more. I needed to know everything about her gift if I ever hoped to defeat her.

And she happily obliged. "Oh, and that's not all. My senses are enhanced, and I'm stronger and faster than I was before. Also, I adapt, I learn far quicker. I am unstoppable!" She was completing her circle around me, reveling in her power.

"Truly," I said, and meant it. She'd not be an easy foe to beat.

"What did you say?" she hissed, suddenly turning on me. "Did I say you could speak, you bloody whore?" she snapped and slammed the crop into me, over and over. One hit, to my unblemished cheek, turned my head and sent blood spurting into my mouth. If I'd been able to, I would have curled into a ball to protect myself from her wild wrath, but it was over soon enough and she was panting, and shuddering. "Spirits, you're a mess." She giggled. "I need..." She turned and headed for the door. "I need Aaghar and that cock of his!" Her voice was full of heated desire. Apparently, torture made her horny.

She got to the door, unlocked it and before she left, stood for a moment in the doorway, silhouetted by the lantern-light outside. "I'll return, Dawn. You'll not die, not yet, that must be saved to be done before your mother, but you'll suffer. You'll suffer for what your mother did to me." Her breathing was heavy. "And remember, if I return and find you've veered into your avatar and escaped, then everything I'm doing to you, I'll do to that friend of yours, the soft one. Actually, I'll do worse to her. I don't need her like I need you. She'll die painfully, so very painfully." A laugh. "So, stay here my pet, and... suffer..." She drew out the word and laughed as she slammed the door behind her.

I finally had a moment to myself and, with no one around to keep a brave face for, I allowed myself to weep. My wounds stung, and I had no clue how I was going to get out of here. I could veer and escape these bonds, but if I did, I'd not be able to get back into them afterward. And I fully believed Swan's threat to kill

Roo. That meant, if I veered and escaped, I'd have to be certain I could save Roo as well, but I didn't even know where she was. She might not be nearby. Which meant I couldn't risk trying to escape yet, until I had more information. I needed another session of counter-interrogation to find out more. I was not looking forward to it.

I couldn't risk losing Roo. I loved Roo like a sister, like a part of me. Our two avatars were the same and that meant something. We were kindred spirits and the thought that I might inadvertently cause her death — that torturous thought — kept me here and kept me... as Swan had wanted... suffering.

Roo had told me a little of her time in the dungeons of the royal palace of Thraan. She hadn't said much, and I could tell there were still painful memories there. But she had mentioned the feeling of helplessness at knowing she could escape but it might mean the death of those she loved.

I felt that same helplessness now.

CHAPTER 5

ROO

I woke slowly. My mind was addled and my body sore from the beating I'd taken at the hands of Swan's guards. She'd told them not to really hurt me, but to make it clear the sort of pain I'd feel if I tried to escape.

I'd gotten the point.

I groaned as I tried to sit up.

"You're awake? Good." Came a voice from the darkness of my cell. It was a female voice, which I thought I recognized, but couldn't place through the fog of my thoughts.

"Who's there?" I asked. I could hear very well and there was enough light coming in through the small grate high in the door of the cell that my eyes would eventually adjust and see well enough to move around in here. Yet from my hearing alone, I could tell the other person was about a half-dozen feet away, probably sitting. Her breathing was even.

"It's me, Roo. Midnight."

"Midnight?" My mind was still hazy and for a moment the name didn't mean anything to me.

Midnight, of the Royal House, who came west with us, then went after Swan, Leoa said, reminding me.

Midnight! Right! Thank you.

"You... were captured?" I guessed that was why she hadn't stopped Swan from attacking us again.

"Indeed." Her voice indicated she wasn't happy about this. "As were you it seems. Was... was Dawn also caught?" I caught the edge of fear in her voice.

"Yes."

She swore.

"Can't you transform and escape?" I asked. That had been my first thought. I needed to get out of here. I wasn't shackled, but there was a heavy door to this cell, perhaps as a kangaroo-rat I could find a hole to sneak out and get to Dawn and...

"My bat form is tiny, and I could probably fit through those bars, but..."

"But?"

"Once I'm out in the hall, there's nowhere for me to go."

"Oh?" I was curious how she knew that. I shifted, finally able to see enough to find a wall and shuffle over to sit against it. If she couldn't get out as a small bat, then I probably wouldn't have much luck as a small rodent.

"Swan knew my form. She was aware of what I could do, even how big I am in avatar form. This entire block of dungeons has been... well sealed off. There are no holes, no tiny fissures between stones." As she spoke, she too moved, rising to come sit next to me. And at this point she lowered her voice to a bare whisper. "The guards outside can hear us if we speak like that. Let them think we think there is no way out."

"So, there is one?" I whispered back hopefully.

"Well... no. but I've slowly been making one. It's not easy as a bat, or even as a person, clawing away at the mortar between stones. I've only managed to get about two inches deep so far. I think I've got another three or four to go to get through that wall, if there is indeed a room or hall on the other side. Though even if there is nothing on the other side but dirt and earth, I could also dig through that... but I think you would dig through it faster in your form, yes?"

That was probably true, rats were natural burrowers through... all sorts of materials. "Where is it?" I asked, keeping my voice low.

Midnight grasped my hand, and we rose together. She guided me to a spot not far away along the wall, running my fingers along the joint between stones to a hole.

"Let me see what I can do," I said and veered into

my avatar form. The hole was tight for me, but I squeezed into it. It wasn't comfortable, but I found the end and began chipping away at the mortar with teeth and claws. I made a dent, but little more than that and squirmed out backwards. I shifted back.

"I can burrow through it, yes, but that mortar is hard and I probably won't get through quickly."

Midnight sighed. "I feared that might be the case." I heard the faint swish of her hair as she shook her head and the grinding of her teeth. "Pits." Then a heavy breath. "If it had just been me in here, I wouldn't mind the time taken to escape, but every minute we're in here is another minute Dawn is probably suffering at the hands of that maniac." Realizing she'd raised her voice a little, she hushed herself again. "Any other thoughts on how to get out of here quickly?"

She was asking me?

You are resourceful and have abilities she does not. She may have considered many options already, but another perspective never hurts. Leoa was stalwart and certain. *I for one think that shifting and trying to get out into the hall, at least to look around might not be a bad idea.*

True, thanks. I thought about it for a minute. There was something only I could do. I could use my spirit-gift to affect the emotions of the guards somehow, but first I needed to know: "How many guards are there?" I made sure to keep my voice low.

"Four, two just outside our door, another two on

this side of the door at the end of the hall, which leads out of this corridor." It sounded like she'd already scouted the hall herself. If her avatar could fit between the bars of the small opening in the door, then she might have been able to peek out and see what was out there.

Four guards. "Could you... take them, if they were in here and... confused?"

I heard a huff of breath. "I'm weak. I haven't eaten much for... however long I've been in here. But... I could easily take two if you took the other two."

"I... don't fight... not well anyway. Could you take all four? I can make them confused and with no real spirit to fight."

"Then... maybe?" She didn't sound certain. "I'm willing to try. What will you do exactly?"

"I'd manipulate their emotions to get them in here, then once they are, drain their emotions away, leave them empty with just a touch of confusion. I've done it before."

"And you're certain you could do four."

I'd done something similar to the myriad creatures on the shores of the Oseran Lake. Instead of confusion, I'd sought to calm them. But I'd been well rested and strong then. I was weak and aching now, but still... it shouldn't be a problem. "Yes."

She laughed a little. "I heard a hint of uncertainty in that 'yes,' but since I'm not entirely certain I can fight them… I won't fault you for your own uncertainty. Let's do this."

I nodded and rose, going to the door.

On my tiptoes, I could just barely see out the small barred grate, but still that angle wasn't good enough to see the guards in the hall. I dropped back down.

Which emotion would get them in here? Fear would probably drive them away. Anger, if it was strong enough, might get them in here to try to rough us up a little. But would there be an easier way, a different emotion? The trick would be taking them from their extreme emotion down to nothing quickly. If the emotion I used wasn't as intense as anger, then that part might be easier.

What about something like curiosity? Leoa suggested. *Make some strange noises in here and pique their interest.*

Yes! That's perfect, thank you!

I went back to Midnight, and whispered: "Start scratching at the wall, loudly, I want them to think we're doing something we're not supposed to, and if they call out, don't answer. I'm going to spike their curiosity so they'll want to come in an investigate."

She nodded.

I went back to the door and waited.

When I heard Midnight's hacking scrape at the wall, I wondered at it myself for a moment. Had she found a stone? It seemed louder than I would have expected if it was just her nails.

Reaching out to the four men in the halls, two closer, two farther off, I seeded their curiosity, then began to build it slowly.

"Hey, what are you doing in there?" one called.

"Stop that or we'll come in and stop you!" another shouted.

I pushed the curiosity of the two who were farther away.

"What's happening?" I heard a more distant voice.

"Can't you hear that? They're scraping at something."

I heard footfalls of the two more distant guards approaching. Good.

Then once they were all close, I pushed their curiosity up another notch. To add to the charade, I whispered: "Keep going, you're almost through!" I was close to the door so I knew the guards would hear it.

"Dragon's tits!" one guard hissed. And I heard the clank of keys, I rushed over to Midnight.

"Get ready," I whispered.

"I am," she said.

The door was opened, and two guards rushed in, lantern in hand. The other two stayed behind at the door. I then had a disorienting moment as I tried to quell the emotion of those inside the cell to nothing, while spiking the curiosity of those still outside, I needed them to come in too.

Midnight moved... though, even in the lantern

light, I couldn't see her; I heard her. I'd forgotten that her spirit-gift was going unnoticed. One of the guards in the cell doubled over, with a painful sounding grunt, then collapsed to the floor with a groan. The other was wary and curious and afraid, I pushed those emotions down to make him empty and confused. He stood there a bit stunned as his head snapped to one side and he collapsed.

"Hey! What's going on?" one of the guards outside shouted.

I pushed harder at their curiosity, pushing down their anxiety. One stepped into the cell. He went flying through the air in a summersault and landed hard on his back, going still.

For the last one I pushed all his emotions down, emptying him, leaving only that touch of confusion. He hesitated long enough for Midnight to reach him. He flew back into the wall of the hall outside, then he doubled over, collapsing like the first one. Not all of them were dead, and some were starting to regain themselves. I pushed relaxation and peace hard upon them. The men sighed as one, then seemed to still.

Getting up, I went to the door.

That worked? Leoa sounded surprised. *I mean... yay! That worked.*

I felt the same way, stunned and joyous at the same time.

Midnight appeared in the hall, then dragged the

one in the hall into the cell and closed the door behind her, retrieving the keys. She smiled. "That worked wonders. Now, let's find Dawn and get out of here, shall we?"

I couldn't agree more.

CHAPTER 6

DAWN

My ears twitched at a sound I couldn't identify at first. It took me a moment to realize it was someone nearby collapsing to the ground... then soft footfalls.

I looked up as the door to my cell opened and there was Roo... and Midnight!

I blinked, a little stunned, unsure if this were reality or some pain-fever-dream.

"Dawn?" I knew that voice, knew it like it belonged to my spirit-sister.

"Oh, Spirits!" And I knew that voice too, its owner had always watched over me as a child.

They were here, they were actually here! I smiled, or tried to. With both cheeks bloodied, it hurt like The Pits to smile. "Ona? Roo?" I croaked, sounding... well about as good as I felt, which wasn't good.

"No!" Roo breathed, putting her hands over her mouth.

Did I look that bad? Well, yeah, probably.

"Get her out of those manacles, I can't reach them," Midnight said handing keys to Roo, who rushed over to me.

"Hold on, we'll get you out of here soon."

Midnight came to my side and when my manacles were unlocked — as much as I wanted to be strong enough to stand on my own — I collapsed into her arms. My arms were wrenched and sore, my one leg would be a massive bruise soon, and could barely hold me up.

"I'll carry you," Midnight said softly.

"Let me make it easier." My voice was rough, breaking. I veered into my avatar and Midnight cupped me in her two hands. She nodded.

"Let's get out of here," Roo said and the two of them hurried to the door.

As they crept through the halls, Midnight whispered: "We'll move faster as ourselves, but quieter and into more places as our avatars. Once we're out of the dungeons, we should veer."

Roo nodded to that, and with her ability to calm and subdue men, we passed out of the dungeons without a fight.

Once we were in the main house, I recognized the corridors of the Estate in Surrin Town.

Midnight veered into a bat and began scouting the halls. Roo set me down, then was another identical form next to me. It was odd. While in an avatar form, it was impossible to speak the human tongue. I could understand others, but not reply. And I was used to that... feeling of being alone. But when Roo and I were transformed together, the squeaks and chirps we voiced were easy enough for us both to understand.

"This way," I said. "I've been here before. I think I know the way out!"

Roo nodded her little rodent head.

Please Amya, give me the strength to move, to run, to get out of this horrid place.

Yes, I am here, I'll give you everything I have. Amya sounded worried, but also hopeful now that we were on the run. He couldn't heal me, but Lumani could lend some of their energy in the form of physical strength, which would help me to overcome my pain and scamper along in my avatar form.

I scurried along, remembering the way back to that sitting room where the group of us had entered the estate when saving Prince Estian. Though it seemed to take a lot longer to get there on these tiny legs.

Midnight rejoined us and in her small bat form was able to slip under the door like we did.

We returned to ourselves, and I slumped into one of the large chairs as we took a moment to regroup before heading outside. Bright light shone in from the windows of the room. It was daytime.

I hoped we had a moment, because I was still in so much pain and just wanted to rest.

"What's the plan?" I asked.

"Get you and get out." Roo shrugged. "We hadn't thought much further than that."

Midnight shrugged and nodded.

"There is a lot of lawn out there, and a lot of guards," I said. "Crossing it as ourselves would be dangerous. Crossing as our avatars will take time, but would probably be safer."

"I'll be well enough," Midnight said. "I can fly and get over the wall, but I won't be able to take you. And I'm not leaving you until you're safe. Did you want to wait until dark?" she asked. "The longer we delay the greater chance someone will—"

As if summoned by her words my keen ears picked up a distant shout: "Prisoners have escaped!" The call was echoed around us through the estate and into the yard.

"Well, Pits." Midnight sighed. "We can't wait." She looked at me with such a pained expression. "Are you sure you'll be well enough to make it out?"

"She will," Roo said, coming to kneel next to me. Roo looked roughed up herself, covered in bruises and small cuts. Yet she smiled and took my hand and a moment later, I felt a surge of hope and determination.

It wasn't physical strength, but it helped me work past my pain.

I blinked and smiled. "Yes, I will, thank you, sister."

And I'll give you everything I have as well, Amya added.

Midnight nodded. "I can remain unseen, so I'll be able to keep an eye on you. I'll be nearby if you need me." She opened the window then vanished.

Roo helped me up, then we went to the window and veered as we reached it, hopping from the sill down to the ground. Once there, I looked around, though my eyes were a little overwhelmed at the moment. Kangaroo-rats were nocturnal and had big eyes for seeing in the dark, but with this much light out, I was having to squint. Luckily, my ears told me everything I needed to know. Guards were pouring out of the house, there were easily fifty men in the yard and their numbers were growing. I didn't know if they knew to be looking for small rodents. Swan didn't know our avatars, but she would know we could shift into animals and the guards might be aware of that as well. Still, we'd have some advantage in these small forms, less likely to be noticed.

I listened to find any pattern to the guard's movements, but there was no predictable guard rotation. They were spreading out across the yard, everywhere and...

No... they weren't everywhere. There was one part

of the yard they were avoiding, and by the heavy huffs of massive breaths from that part of the yard, I thought I knew why... a dragon slept there. No one wanted to risk the wrath of that massive beast, who might snap a man up as a light snack.

Which meant... that was where we needed to go. I turned to Roo and communicated this, then looked up to where I thought Midnight was, and began moving.

We crept along, keeping to the base of the outer wall of the house, until we came to the corner of the manor which was closest to where the dragon slept. There would be a short stretch of yard we'd have to pass through where men might see us, before we got to the large area the guards were avoiding.

I considered making a run for it, but kangaroo-rats didn't so much run, as hop, and that high-speed-hopping might be noticeable. So, I chose a slow creep through the grasses of the lawn.

It seemed to take forever, crossing that small patch of yard, starting and stopping as men drew near. The hardest thing was staying still when heavy booted feet clomped by close enough that I felt the dirt beneath me tremble. It was like dodging giants.

But, eventually, with my tiny heart thundering, I made it into the area where no one dared go.

And a part of me felt relieved, but another part... felt like I'd gone from a boiling pot into the fire itself. I was now in the 'lair' of a dragon and there was a reason men didn't roam here. I just had to hope that my tiny form would not disturb this massive beast. And massive it was. When I'd been in human form, Eophon had been incredibly large. Aaghar's dragon was larger by a factor of two or three. And to something the size of a tiny rodent, the form seemed more like a mountain range than a living being.

"What do you think?" I asked Roo in our avatar speak. "Do we go around the head or the tail?" I posed the same question to Amya. I was worried that getting closer to the head would provide a greater — if still slim — possibility of us being noticed. Yet one twitch of that massive tail and we'd be crushed.

"Tail," Roo said. I agreed, it was less of a risk.

Agreed, Amya added.

Off we went, moving slowly, creeping through the grasses as we began the long trek around the dragon.

There were a few twitches of that mountainous form as we sneaked around it, but nothing significant and — though it took some time — we got to the wall of the compound on the other side of the beast.

I turned to Roo. "We'll need to transform. We should do it together and then leap as one, to get over the wall. There is a good chance someone will spot us, so we should be ready to revert to this form even as we fall on the other side. I think we'll be safe, once we're in the city."

She nodded to this.

I counted down from three and we both acted on: "One."

I shifted to my human form and leapt. Even with one sore and weak leg, I could easily make the jump over the twelve-foot wall. Roo was right there with me.

I had forgotten one small piece of information, having spent so long in my avatar form... I had been naked when I'd gone into it, which meant I was naked now as well.

And whether it was the sudden movement or the appearance of a leaping naked woman... there were shouts from guards behind us as we crested the wall and began the fall on the other side.

I reverted to my avatar form and landed easily, despite the long fall. Roo remained close, transformed as well.

The time for slow stealth was over, so I bolted, hop-running as fast as my small form could go, across the street and into an alley. But I didn't stop there, I kept going, moving from shadow to shadow, away from the estate.

Then the earth below me shook as a horrible roar went up from somewhere behind me. And my keen ears picked up the heavy flap of wings in the distance.

Midnight's voice nearby caught me off-guard in my jittery state. "The dragon comes. Do we run or hide?"

Good question. There would be no way to outrun that beast. But I wanted to get out of the town. Out in the fields it would be easier to burrow down for safety and hide. So... I ran.

"Running it is," Midnight said and a moment later I heard the flap of her tiny wings.

Roo kept pace with me as we darted through the streets and alleys.

The one problem with being outside the city was... if the dragon was going to breathe fire, it would be able to do so freely across the countryside and I didn't know how deep we'd have to burrow to avoid it.

Then, I felt a gust of heat wash over me as a howling blast of fire tore through the town somewhere behind me.

Well apparently, it wasn't even safe in the town. The dragon lord was destroying Surrin Town in his attempt to find us. No. With blasts of fire like that, he wasn't trying to find us. He was trying to kill us.

That got me moving even faster.

The dragon flew low over the alley down which we scurried. I heard the heavy flap of those leathery wings above me. I also heard the keening cry of Swan upon the dragon. She must be riding with the dragon lord. "You'll die for this, Dawn. I'll kill you and your friend and your friend's friends and everyone you ever loved!"

I didn't find her words particularly threatening, since she'd been going to do that anyway. I'd rather die free, with a chance of getting away, than be killed in front of my own mother.

Fire blasted down ahead of us in a long arc.

I paused then.

Tiny wing-flaps announced Midnight's presence, but she didn't transform, the small bat hopped along next to us in the shadows of the alley.

I hesitated. With that blaze ahead of us, we couldn't go forward, and...

I heard another blast of fire as the dragon moved... around the edges of the town. I nodded to myself. They were blocking any way out of the town, creating a wall of fire. And I highly suspected once the edge of the town was ringed with fire... the rest of the town would be burned, outside in. They might even be crazy enough to destroy the estate with all their own guards still trapped there.

Spirits, this was insane.

But it wasn't surprising.

Then, while the dragon was on the far side of the city, making its way around, burning a ring around the town, I heard another sound... the harsh cry... of a falcon.

Hope surged. I didn't know if it was just any falcon or... or *my* Falcon, but I had to believe he'd come looking for me, for us. But... how could I signal him, tell him where we were? His eyes were keen, but he'd have to be looking in the right spot. Whatever I did, I had to act fast, before the dragon returned.

Bloody Bones. I didn't know what to do, so I went

with my first instinct. Transforming back into a person, I ran out from the alley, to the middle of the nearby street. Not much more than two dozen paces away, the fire raged, and its heat radiated out to me. I was naked and drew more than a few glances from the people running through the streets.

I waved my arms, making as big a signal as I could. And I saw the falcon turn... and dive. I pointed to the alley, then ran back into it and veered back into my avatar form.

The falcon landed nearby and hopped along until it saw the three of us. Then, as I'd so desperately hoped, it transformed into a man. In that moment, he was the most beautiful and amazing man I'd ever seen. His dark eyes danced as he flashed a cocky grin. "I can't believe I found you. I'll transform back and carry you out." He veered, then carefully plucked up Roo and I in his claws. Falcon surged up into the sky. Midnight flew somewhere behind us, quickly being left behind.

We flew up and over the fire and were soaring out over the countryside as the dragon completed its circuit of the town. Then, as I'd predicted, they began burning their way inward.

We landed in a small copse of trees, far enough from the town that the roar of the dragon was only a distant thing.

Transforming back to ourselves, Roo and I hugged Falcon fiercely and he did the same.

"I'm so glad to see you!" he said, weeping openly with joy and relief. "I..."

I stopped his mouth with a kiss, then Roo did. We all knew what had happened and how horrid it had been, no need to say it; not yet at least.

"We should move on, quickly," Midnight said, appearing in the woods with us.

Falcon started, but calmed quickly once he saw her.

"Agreed," I said. I was ecstatic to see Falcon, but... I desperately wished to see the others as well. Pan had been dying when I'd last seen him and I had no clue what had befallen Rhino or Ceph or Lyran.

"We're all well enough," Falcon said to calm my nerves. "Though... Ceph burned himself out healing us all."

"Spirits, no!" Roo breathed, covering her mouth with her hands.

Agreed, that wasn't good news. Still, everyone was alive, and *that* was the best news I'd heard all day.

CHAPTER 7

RHINO

We should have been rejoicing, Dawn and Roo had returned to us. But too much horror and loss hung over us. The women were deeply shaken by their captivity. Even the legendary Midnight was quiet and sullen. We all shared a miserable, cloying despair. We'd failed.

Ceph and Lyran were still healing. It had been pure luck that Falcon had found the women while scouting. We hadn't even made plans to rescue them yet. They'd rescued themselves. I should have known they would. They were resilient; fighters.

But still, we were somber and silent around our little fire that evening. It was Dawn herself who eventually broke the stillness.

"I'm curious," Dawn asked, looking at Midnight.

"How long had you been in those dungeons? When were you captured?"

Midnight sighed, clearly not fond of retelling the tale of her failure. "I followed Swan for months, a winding route westward. She seemed to have no direction or purpose. I don't know if she was searching for you or simply wandering. Then... about a month ago, she came to Surrin Town and met with the dragon lord. I... I got overconfident, or... I don't know. I didn't know the extent of Swan's power. I thought myself safe, sneaking around the estate to spy on her and the dragon lord, but... somehow, she knew I was there. She trapped me in a bubble of something I couldn't see. Perhaps it was air itself, because she then seemed to deprive me of air to breathe and I fell unconscious. When I woke, I was in that dungeon. She knew my avatar form and had made sure there was no way out for me. I was left there to die. As a Fey, and as a True-Bonded, I had reserves of strength and fortitude, but I was nearly done with them by the time you found me. Another week, perhaps two and I would have starved to death."

Dawn's head was hanging, and I thought I knew why.

"I... If I'd known..." She looked up at Midnight with a horrible sorrow and pain in her gaze. "We were in those dungeons, rescuing the prince of Basia a week or so before we were captured. I... I could have helped you... I should have looked through more cells. I'm sorry Midnight."

Midnight gave a sympathetic smile. "There was no way you could have known, don't torture yourself over that."

Dawn flinched at the word torture, but she nodded.

She then asked Pan how he had survived Swan's dagger to his heart. That prompted more of our tales from... that dreadful night. My tale was particularly hard to tell. I'd been so close to defeating Aaghar... and then nearly died. The others made sounds of understanding, of sympathy, but how could they understand? I had stood up to the man, matched him blow for blow, and with one more strike I could have ended all of this... one strike. And because I hadn't, so many others had suffered.

We were quiet and barely spoke the next day, resting and regaining ourselves still. Ceph had roused and he and Lyran were carried by Eophon to a secluded glade in the forest. But we hadn't moved far from where Eophon had landed. That... turned out to be a mistake.

That night we heard Aaghar's dragon approaching.

We were all terrified. Neither Lyran nor Eophon were up for another dragon fight, despite both being on the mend. They used their ability to remain hidden. The rest of us sought shadows and bushes to do the same. That massive dragon circled over us several times, but thankfully didn't see us. When they left, we slunk out from our hiding and quickly fled the area. We kept moving, terrified, after that. We spent long days slogging through the forest and restless nights with no fire, huddled in fear. We headed east, after the rest of our forces, now long ahead of us and potentially scattered to the four winds.

After a week of running — and not having seen Aaghar since that night — we thought ourselves far enough away that we risked fires and warmth. Oddly it was Dawn and Roo who seemed to recover their spirits before the rest of us, and once we'd felt safe enough to do so, they began to get... reacquainted with us, spending time, one-on-one, with each of us. Though, I was one of the last to see them.

Which gave me lots of time during those evenings alone to brood and sink ever deeper into my self-loathing.

At first, I couldn't believe I'd come that close to defeating Aaghar, but then I realized I hadn't been close at all. As much as I had hit him two of the three times he'd agreed upon... they had been shallow hits. And... perhaps he'd just been playing with me. Perhaps he wouldn't have given up and the entire thing had been a ruse. If so, I hadn't been anywhere near defeating him. And even if he'd kept his promise and fled after three hits... I was certain those minor wounds wouldn't have hindered him much. He'd have lived to terrorize more people.

None of this thinking is getting you anywhere, Iomu chided me.

Don't you think I know that! I shouted at my Lumani. I didn't want to hear anything she had to say. I wasn't strong, despite my size. I was inexperienced and — in so many ways — barely more than a child. As much as I'd been in many fights these past few months and learned a lot, I knew now, I was still a novice. There was so much I didn't know.

Then do something about it! Train. Get better for the next time. Iomu didn't give up easily. *Stop pouting, you big lug.*

Yeah, that's not helping. I knew she was right; I *was* pouting, but that only made me feel worse, falling into a deeper depression.

I forced myself to train with Lyran whenever we had a moment. He was the most experienced of us all. But I wasn't in a good place mentally, and his lessons didn't seem to sink in. I just kept losing to him... and in my mind I was losing to Aaghar again... over and over.

I wanted to train with someone who wasn't a dragon lord, but Ceph was our next most experienced warrior and he'd fallen into a terrible mire of despair after the loss of his gift. Even his time with Roo hadn't healed him of these dire moods. Apparently, she'd just held him as he trembled and wept. Something told me there was more going on with him, than just the loss of his gift, but since he wouldn't talk to any of us, we weren't sure how to help him.

Perhaps you need to get your mind off fighting for a while? Iomu suggested. She seemed at her wits end. It couldn't have been easy dealing with me.

But the only thing which distracted me from thinking of my failure as a warrior, was thoughts of being with Dawn and Roo. I needed to be with the women I loved. I so desperately wanted to lose myself in their embrace, feel the full-body climax that came comingled with their shuddering and gasping orgasm. And when my evening with Dawn finally came, my cock ached with painful need as we kissed and undressed each other. When my erection was revealed, she gasped. "Spirits, I'd forgotten how huge you are." I was so tall and she so short that my erection brushed the bottom of her chin. She reached up to stroke me and I clenched my teeth as her touch nearly made me come.

"Please," I gasped, breathless.

"Oh," she said softly. "Are you..."

"I need you," I begged. But more than that, I wanted to fill her, like I had the last time we'd been together. I wanted Ceph to change her so I could thrust all the way up under those small but full tits. But Ceph couldn't do that any longer. Though... "I want Pan to be with us," I breathed, edging so close to my climax as she stroked me. "I want to fill you like I did last time." I met her golden-eyed gaze and growled. "I want to own you, be your master, screw your brains out." I knew she liked that sort of talk. I also remembered the haze of ascendancy I'd felt that time she'd let me be her 'master.' She certainly hadn't minded and — from her own account — had had a body and mind-shattering orgasm. But still, if I didn't want to hurt her then we needed Pan.

And yet... her gaze turned hard. "Rhino... no." Her tone was firm.

"Yes, we need Pan," I said insistent. "I don't want to be restrained. I want to lose myself inside you." Then I added, only partially playfully: "That is a command from your master."

She released my cock from her stroking and stepped back, clearly irritated. "Right now, I don't want a master," she said firmly. "After what Swan did, I've had enough of people having power over me. I love the idea of some rough sex with you, but I've had enough pain recently. That's not what I want right now. If you want to feel fully inside me, then have Pan shrink that prick of yours down to a reasonable size. How's that sound?"

My jaw tightened. I didn't want to be smaller. I wanted the be all of my powerful, massive self. "No. I—"

Her small hand hit my chin harder than I was

expecting, the slap turning my head. She'd had to stand on her tiptoes to even reach me.

"Then you can go jerk off in the woods for all I care," she fumed, turning away. "When you're willing to be reasonable, come to me. Until then you're getting none of this." She vaguely motioned to herself. She didn't even turn back as she walked away.

I let out a howl of frustration.

I didn't know which hurt more, the pain of her leaving me, or the agony of my desperate cock. As much as I didn't want to do as she'd said, I needed the release, so I went into the woods and stroked myself. I grew violent with need as time passed, but I just couldn't come. All I did was rub myself raw, only adding to my pain. I cried out into the night once again, as my uncertain soul folded in on itself.

I'd pushed Dawn away. I'd wanted too much from her. I was disgusted with myself and my need to feel powerful. Yet, even knowing that didn't help. It didn't lesson the pent-up resentment and anger within me.

Even Iomu was quiet. I felt her sighs and the impression of her shaking her head, but she said nothing. That was probably a good thing, I wouldn't have been kind to her if she'd said much of anything.

I only hoped Dawn would have me back, that I hadn't ruined our relationship. But first... I needed to figure myself out. The trouble was, I had no idea how to do that. I felt like the only way to feel powerful again was to defeat Aaghar, to find him and fight him. But that was just a man-brained fantasy.

Roo found me a little later that evening. I hadn't returned to the others, and she'd come looking.

"Dawn told me what happened," she said tenderly, laying a hand on my arm. "And I can feel the turmoil within you, the anger and fear and uncertainty. What do you need, Rhino?"

I almost yelled at her, just because I wanted to yell at someone. But she was so full of love and tenderness I couldn't do it. But that left me with a massive pent-up malignancy of emotion, which I didn't know how to express. I didn't know what to do; didn't know what I needed.

With Roo here now, my cock was already swelling again, desperate. But my thoughts and feelings were still a haze of need to command, to own, to impose myself upon her. It was becoming clear to me that my inability to defeat Aaghar had turned into a need to dominate the women I loved. And as much as I knew that wasn't the right answer, I still wanted it. I was stuck between my irrational desires and my love for Dawn and Roo.

Finally, my writhing emotions gave way to bitter tears, but I despised every salty drop that traced my cheek. I just didn't know what to do, how to get passed this. All I wanted in that moment was to take Roo in my arms and plunge my cock into her until I finally had a release! But I knew I couldn't, not with how things had gone with Dawn.

Roo, tender as ever, took my hand and led me out of the forest back to one of the two blanketed bowers where we'd been having our encounters. She put her fingers under my chin, then raised my head until my gaze met hers... and I was surprised at the carnal hunger I saw there.

"Dawn is fragile right now," she said, voice hushed and husky as she began to undo the laces on her dress. "Neither her spirit nor her body could handle your... fervor." Her voice grew quieter, throaty, her breath coming quickly. "But I can." Her dress fell away, revealing all of her glorious, lush, body.

By the Spirits! Was she truly offering herself to me?

"I will still need some... warming up," she said.

I needed no further encouragement. I grabbed her and laid her on the ground, then kissed my way quickly down her body, lingering a moment on those glorious, large breasts, sucking a heavy nipple into my mouth, making her moan. Then I kissed my way down between her legs.

I was not soft nor subtle, but she didn't seem to mind. I devoured her folds, tongue forcefully pressing into her, wetting her as she gasped and groaned. I sucked and nibbled on her clitoris, feeling her hips rise to meet my lips as her passion mounted. And once she was piqued, I doused my hands in oil. One pressed to her, fingers penetrating her opening to ensure she was well ready for me. My other hand lathered my cock. Still, I waited, massaging her further with my fingers, curling them, driving them up into her special spot. She came, wetting my hands, her fluids mixing with the oil. Still, I ensured I could get at least three of my thick fingers inside her before I knew she was ready.

"Yes," she breathed, "Give me your cock!" She lifted her hips, angling up her wet and ready opening. I was trembling from keeping my own release in check for so long. I positioned myself, moving slowly at first, making sure my thick tip was inside her. Then I thrust hard to fill her.

She cried out, body arching and tensing, even as the force of my thrust pushed her along the blankets. I hadn't gotten fully inside her, but then... I should have known I wouldn't. I'd gotten so used to Ceph or Pan manipulating the women so I could be deep and fully inside them. Without that... I could never be as fully inside her as I wished to be. I thrusted hard again, hoping perhaps I could get deeper, but again, she cried out, writhing with an orgasm as I simply pushed her along the ground.

I nearly wept with frustration. I needed desperately to feel that enfolding warmth, but I couldn't. I thrusted again and again, no longer seeking to be deep, but just wanting to feel the way she moved around me. With every push, I filled her fully and pressed so deep she cried out with something that sounded like a mix of pain and pleasure, which seemed to be everything she needed to bring her to her next orgasm.

I finally stopped, propped on my arms over her, weeping. I was still aching for a release, painfully built up to an extreme, but unable to get what I needed. My soul ached at not being fulfilled. And with how hard I'd been, I had to ask: "Did I hurt you?"

Roo gasped. "No, I'll be well. That was... and you're still...?"

"I just can't get as deep as I want. I want to feel your warmth all around this blasted huge cock of mine, and I can't." I pulled out of her quickly and she gasped again. I turned away, kneeling, hiding my tears from her.

I felt her warm hand on my broad back. "Rhino..." she whispered and soothing peace seeped into me from where she touched. "I think I might know a way to give you what you seek, but first... could we... talk?"

I didn't turn, just nodded. I'd do anything.

Her hand began to stroke my back. "I love you," she whispered and it nearly broke me. I let out an embarrassing loud sob. "And I can feel the torment in your soul. But you have to know that this one defeat doesn't define you. You *are* strong, stronger than almost any other man in this world. Yet, it is a strange rule of fate and life, that there is always someone stronger. Even for those who are the strongest, others will always be trying to challenge them and eventually, someone younger and stronger will defeat them. Someone will even defeat Aaghar someday. It may be you or it may not be. The point is, your strength isn't what defines who you are. Nor does your ability to win battles. It's what's in your heart that defines you, Rhino, what you love, what you seek with all your passion and desire, that is who you are."

"But... what... do I seek?" I asked, still sniffling. Could she read into my emotions and see?

I know what you seek, Iomu said softly.

You do? I was curious. Iomu was rarely insightful. She was usually the wild one prompting me to fight and face all manner of dangers. Yet her voice now was softer, tender.

She let out a bit of a laugh. *I love your strength Rhino, and if my host were your lover, like Roo and Dawn, I'd want to feel all of your power.* I felt her shudder with a bit of ecstasy. *But Roo is right. That is just... your body. I've been with you long enough now to see your soul. And it's clear to me, you seek to protect. You did it as a shepherd, but that wasn't enough. You've done it with Dawn and Roo and all of these others, but even that isn't enough. You... we... need to protect everyone we can, Rhino, that is what you seek with all your heart and soul.*

But I wasn't able to—

Shut up and listen, you lug. Women are talking. Always

listen when women are talking; they know more than you do! I could tell shew as fed up with my self-scorn.

I laughed a little inwardly at her rebuke. *I'm listening.*

You were about to say you weren't able to protect people that night, when you fought Aaghar? Well, I beg to differ. You slaughtered hundreds of men, even the commanders. You probably put their army into disarray. That night we were meant to be protecting the refugees, and we did. Even delaying Aaghar was enough to help them get away. You DID protect people that night and you were willing to do it until the very end. That is valiant and noble, and I love that about you... you big lug.

This time my laugh made it to the outside, as I breathed a faint chuckle.

"Did Iomu help you?" Roo asked. "I sense you're feeling a bit better."

"I am, yes. Iomu helped me realize I need to protect others and that that's exactly what I did that night. I didn't fail."

Roo kissed my back lightly. "No... you didn't." There was still that husky sensuousness to her voice and I turned, wiping away the wetness on my cheeks. She looked up at me, ignoring my tears. "Now... like I said, I think I have a way for you to feel fully embraced by me. Would you like that?"

"Spirits, yes!" I gasped, pleading.

Roo grabbed one of the blankets on the ground, as

well as the bottle of oil, and said: "Follow me." She led me into the forest. Luckily it didn't take her long to find what she was looking for, the stump of a tree. She threw the blanket over it and sat upon it. She dribbled some oil over her breasts then began to massage it into the soft curves, and I nearly exploded watching. Then she looked up at me, eyes hooded with desire. "Come to me."

I did.

She opened her legs so I could stand between them, then she grabbed my butt to draw me closer. My thick cock slid easily between her oiled breasts, and she ducked her head down to fill her mouth with my tip. Then she pushed at the sides of her breasts, pressing their warmth around me.

I shivered with anticipation, finally feeling her warmth fully around me. I began soft thrusts between her breasts up into her mouth.

"Yes," she whispered between thrusts. "Take what... you need."

I was already aching to come, I didn't need much. My thrusts grew harder. I put a hand on the back of her head, not forcing her down, but keeping her just in the right spot to feel that wet warmth of her mouth around my tip as I ended my thrusts. And when — with a wordless cry into the night — I came, I felt her mouth close around me, her lips and tongue urging my release, her breasts pressing close around my twitching shaft. I was finally able to pierce the pain of my longing and feel the fullness of a true and body-clenching orgasm with this amazing woman.

After, we found a stream and cleaned ourselves. As we did Roo spoke softly: "You need to apologize to Dawn."

"I know." I sighed heavily. I reached over to Roo, smoothing her hair down over her neck and shoulders. "Thank you, for... everything tonight. I needed it."

"It was you and Iomu who did the hard work, I just let you... screw my brains out..." She looked at me and smiled mischievously. Spirits! Having my heated words to Dawn thrown back at me by one as soft and kind as Roo was just... wrong.

I'm fairly certain I blushed then.

She laughed lightly. I joined her after a moment. It felt so very good to laugh and I felt even more of the pent-up tension inside me release. It would still take me a while to regain my confidence, but now I knew I could do it.

And I knew I had two wonderful women in my life to help me. Women who were far stronger than I was... where it counted.

CHAPTER 8

LYRAN

"I'm worried about Ceph," I said as Roo lay in my arms after a passionate evening of love and sweat. "Actually, I'm worried about... all of us." I stroked her hair and her back as she lay with her head upon my chest. "Ceph is listless, lifeless. I know he lost his gift, but I sense there is more he's not telling us. Rhino seems better now, after you spoke with him, but I can still see in his eyes the wounds upon his soul. Pan has been quiet and reserved, though that's not much of a change for him, but after what happened I think he bears some scars as well. The twins won't stop talking, but they're not really talking about anything important. They seem to have somehow closed themselves off from the rest of us."

Roo sighed heavily. "You're very perceptive. All of what you say is true. I can sense their emotions and everyone is... all over the place, since the battle in the forest. Pan is confused and uncertain, Rhino is better but still struggling with feelings of inadequacy. The twins have pulled away as you say, and Ceph... Ceph feels empty." She shuddered. "I've forced that feeling on others from time to time, but never have I ever felt anyone who'd brought it upon themselves. I have no clue what he's going through. He won't talk, he only weeps. I do what I can. I've tried to push hope and love into him, but his soul is like some vast void, sucking in what I give him and reducing it to nothing. I've never felt anything like it before." She began to tremble. "Spirits, I don't want to think about this now, this was supposed to be our time, a pleasant time, a time to be with you and forget about everything else!" She seemed on the verge of tears.

"Then I will help you forget," I whispered, and quickly rolled over onto her, pressing my mouth to hers in a passionate kiss. It took her a moment of confusion before she was responding to me in kind, heated, passionate, full of need to be distracted by this moment.

I'd thought myself thoroughly spent from our previous session, having already come twice myself — and I'd lost track of her orgasms so far — but she was an amazing woman, sensual and alive with love and sexual energy. I found my semi-aroused cock growing, hardening, as I anticipated yet another round of passion with her.

When our lips parted next, I whispered: "What do you need, whatever it is, I'll give it to you."

I saw in her expression what I'd felt in her kiss: a simple need to be elevated beyond the cares of the world.

"Something… different?" she said, just a little uncertain. "Something I'll have to concentrate on, something wild and fun and sexy and mind-blowing."

A tall order, but I thought I could accommodate.

Needing a moment to consider this request I returned to kissing her, but this time moved down to pleasure the fullness of her breasts with my lips as I brought a hand down between her legs to begin rousing her folds once more. She was still wet from our previous lovemaking, and I quickly got her juices flowing again.

"Yes," she whispered to me as I plucked up a nipple in my lips, sucking hard upon the puckered flesh, and raking my teeth over the towering nub. And it was then that inspiration hit me. There was a lot one could do with their mouth. And there was a position I'd heard of but never tried. I'd read about it, in an old text one of my older brothers had brought home from the far-west, a book depicting sexual positions and apparently — though none of us could read it — telling of the possible pleasures men and women could achieve. It would be a challenging position, but I knew Roo was flexible enough to do it.

Reluctantly, I lifted my lips from her wonderous breasts. "I have an idea for something to try, but it's... adventurous. It requires you to bend backward, literally. Feeling up for it?"

She nodded, eagerly. I saw the heated anticipation in her eyes.

I talked her through it as I moved, rolling onto my back. "Come to me," I said, then for lack of a better way to describe it, I added, "Sit on my face."

She cocked her head and obliged, moving to straddle me, then slowly moving up.

"You're going to need to brace yourself a little. Stick your feet back under my shoulders, so your heels are in my armpits." Describing it didn't sound sexy at all, but she didn't seem to mind.

She laughed. "You say all the sexiest things." Yet she did as instructed. She shifted, her thighs hovering over my face as she slid her feet back under my arms, kneeling above me.

"Now," I said. "You're going to arch backwards. Use your hands to support and guide you. I'll lift my head to pleasure you while you... lean your head back and... take me with your mouth."

She grinned with the twitch of an eyebrow. "Oh, this does sound tricky."

"How deep I go will be mostly up to you, I won't be

thrusting hard. However you want to pleasure me, do so. And I'll concentrate on pleasuring you."

She nodded and did a little dance above me for a moment, hips swaying, arms up in her auburn hair, so seductive and inviting. Then she slowly arched backwards, hands reaching back until they found my raised knees. This helped to get her in place as she walked her hands down my legs to either side of my hips. She didn't have to lean back all the way. I had an exceptionally long cock and she could pleasure my tip without too much strain from this position. I felt one of her hands stroking my still rousing erection and bringing it to her lips. When the wet warmth of her mouth found me, sucking hard for a moment, my cock surged to full arousal and she moaned as it filled her mouth.

I, in turn, lifted my head to press my lips to her slick folds. I tasted her arousal, even our mingled release from our first session. She was sweet and warm, and I dove in with my mouth to pleasure her. I used my arms, alternating between grasping her butt — which helped support her — and reaching around her full thighs to play with her engorged clitoris.

I felt her body trembling, though I didn't know if it was from strain or pleasure, but when I heard her moans and felt the subtle movement of her hips rocking against my face, I knew it wasn't all strain.

And she was working wonders upon me, taking me deep into her throat. She moved through upside-down push-ups to take in my length as she allowed more and more of me into her. By the Sacred Flame that felt amazing!

I wanted to return the favor, redoubling my efforts with tongue, teeth, lips and fingers upon her quivering folds to ensure her release.

And with her mouth well occupied she couldn't cry out, but I did feel her body tense and twitch and shudder with bliss as a rush of her juices wet my lips. I swallowed the sweet gift and pressed in closer, deeper, tongue lashing and licking and pressing into her.

Her legs pressed to either side of my head, squeezing close as I heard a faint whimper from her. She alternated between pleasuring my tip with her tongue and plunging it deep into her mouth. I felt my own release building.

But before I got there, she came again, and this time, so forcefully she pulled herself back up from her back-bend and both her hands went behind my head to press me hard to her as her thighs clamped around me and she shook with tremor after tremor of a violent orgasm, finally able to cry out her repeated bliss.

And when, finally, she released my head — and I was able to breathe again — she pulled herself off me. "That was amazing," she said, gasping. "I... you were... your lips... oh!" She shivered. "And I was able to get your cock so deep in that position, awkward as it was."

She turned and reached down to stroke my cock. "And you didn't get a release. I should give you one."

"This was all for you, I need nothing."

"It was all for me," she agreed with a smile. "And luckily... I'm not done yet." She grinned and grasped my shaft tightly, viciously stroking it from base to tip and back.

"Do as you like," I grunted straining with the pressure she was arousing in me.

"I will," she said with a mischievous grin. She found some oil and began covering my cock in it, and once I was well covered, she poured some on her hand and turned away from me, showing me how she was rubbing it into her back entrance. "Get the hint?" she whispered.

I did.

Moving to kneel behind her, I grabbed the oil, dumping far too much over the glorious round orbs of her buttocks as she bent over, on all fours. I massaged it into her, all over, and then focused down and in to her other entrance, plunging my finger into her. She gasped and moaned, slowly rocking upon my fingers as I got her wet and ready. Then I knelt behind her, one hand on her hip, holding her firm, the other on my cock guiding it. I pressed to the puckered opening and felt its resistance, even with the oil.

"Do it," she breathed, needfully. And I made sure I was well positioned, then grasped her hips with both hands and lunged forward into her. The oil did its job as I filled her, driving deep. She gasped and cried out. But I was far from done.

I brought her legs together and straddled her on the outside. Then as I thrusted with long slow strokes, I slid my oil-slick hands up her body and leaned over her, to feel the weight of her hanging breasts, I covered them with the oil on my hands as I grasped and groped. Then I helped to lift her off her hands, until her back was pressed to my chest. She leaned to one side so our lips could meet, however awkwardly. I continued my assault upon her breasts with firm intensity, my cock throbbing inside her, thrusting harder and harder as I reached my breaking point... for the third time that night. But didn't want to come alone.

I slid a wet hand down her body to her folds. Pressing and rubbing her clitoris, fingers tracing her folds, slick with her previous release. I drove two fingers up into her, curling them as I pressed my palm back upon her clit, rocking it between those two sensitive spots. She whimpered a trembling moan against my lips, then drew back long enough to say: "Come with me!"

I needed no more than that.

I thrusted myself hard and deep and felt my hot release inside of her, as my hands worked furiously at breast and loins to urge her onward to her own point of bliss.

She tensed, with a drawn out: "Yes." Her opening tightened around me, milking my shaft, making me come all the harder, as she shuddered with the thrills of a full-body orgasm.

Even before I was finished, she gasped "thank you," as she slowly relaxed, leaning back against me. "Thank you," she whispered again, repeating it until I was done and we slowly parted. Then I held her close, folding blankets over us, to ensure any painful thoughts or feelings didn't return before she fell into a restful sleep in my arms.

"No," I whispered, kissing the top of her head, even though she was already well asleep. "Thank you."

CHAPTER 9

PAN

We broke through the edge of the Maraslad forest, somewhere along its south-eastern fringes. This land belonged to no kingdom, rough and uninhabited. These were badlands: rocky and barren, rolling hills covered in scrub brush, with rough crags and blind valleys. Lots of good places to hide and where we hoped to find the rest of our army and refugees.

We'd been following the path they'd carved through the forest. So many travelling together had left a clear trail. Though we'd guessed that as they'd travelled, they'd separated out into smaller and smaller groups, as the path had become less defined over the last week or so.

The eight of us stood on the crest of a hill not far from the edge of the forest.

"How far away do you think Elista is?" Roo asked

softly, there was a note of wistfulness in her voice. She was homesick. I didn't blame her. We'd all been away from home and family for some time.

You've been away from your Fey family for even longer, Eona whispered within me. *Do you wish to see them again?*

Yes, some day. I had been waiting until I could go with Dawn by my side. Now... I'll have others as well. A new family.

Yes, these others have grown close, haven't they?

Indeed. I had no brothers growing up, but now I have five. I love them all... and Roo is like a sister.

And Dawn?

Dawn is my truest love. I care not that others are with her, so long as I am one of them. I cherish her, and every moment I spend with her.

Eona gave the impression of a solemn nod. *I am so very glad I Chose you, Pangolin.*

As am I, I said and meant it.

"Not far," Falcon said in response to Roo's question. He and swift had been scouting the skies for us; planning a safe route, while keeping an eye out for survivors, not to mention our foes. Thankfully, we'd not seen any sign of the dragon lord since that one terrifying night after Dawn, Midnight, and Roo had escaped. "In the skies, I could reach north-western Elista in less than a day. Travel the same distance south and you'd be well into eastern Basia. These badlands stretch south and east and become the rocky lands of eastern Elista, around Cragmount. That said, traveling will take much longer on the ground with all these crags and crevices."

I was a little surprised we were so close.

Swift continued his brother's explanation and seemed to answer my unasked question. "Though it may have seemed like we'd been travelling east these past days, it's been more south-east."

"So close," Roo said, that same heavy nostalgia in her voice. Then she sighed heavily. "And yet so far, so much left to do."

And that heaviness weighed on all of us. My sympathetic soul felt the pain of the others, even though I was feeling more robust myself. I'd felt different since healing Eophon: stronger, tougher, enhanced. More than what I had been. Though to any outside viewer, I looked the same as I had. I hadn't wanted to say anything to the others since they were all struggling with much darker things. To talk about my... enhancement, my feelings of power, seemed wrong. So... I waited for the right time to tell them what had happened to me. I didn't know what that would look like, but I figured I'd know it when it happened. The only person I'd mentioned anything to, was Dawn. I'd let her know I felt... different, but in a good way, and not to tell the others. She'd understood.

Falcon and Swift took off once more to scout the

vales and hills around us. The rest of us followed the vague path we had been following, Rhino leading us. He was the best tracker among us, from his days as a herder, tracking down lost sheep.

Lost sheep; it certainly seemed like we'd lost our entire flock. And the unasked question that weighed on all of us was: how many had survived that terrible attack? There had been roughly two thousand refugees, along with an army of thirteen hundred men who'd fought bravely to protect them.

The trail we followed led to a steep-sided canyon. There we found an old game trail, barely passable, down the side of the cliff. We traversed it carefully, people clinging to each other during some of the more perilous bits. If others had come down here... it couldn't have been easy.

Once we were in the shadows of the narrow valley, we found a babbling brook, which we'd been hearing for some time. There we stopped and drank.

"I don't think we have far to go now," Rhino said as the rest of us sat drinking by the river. Dawn and Roo didn't need to drink, but they did, scooping up the clear, clean water in their hands, reveling in the refreshment of it.

"In fact... I think I see others," Rhino whispered.

We all followed Rhino's gaze down the canyon. There, in the distance, was a small group out by the waters. They saw us and waved. Luckily Rhino was a clear and visible indicator they knew well, telling them who we were.

We rose, suddenly excited, and went to see these others.

As we suspected, it was a small group, mostly warriors from Lyran's militia. Some of them were healing from nasty wounds.

"We thought you all dead or captured!" one said.

"Some of us nearly died, and others were captured. We've... changed our fates since then." Lyran was circumspect. The dragon lord wasn't overtly encumbered with dark emotions like the others, but... I think he felt beholden and responsible for Ceph's current doldrums. Ceph had given everything and more to heal him and Lyran was now hale and strong whereas Ceph was a fragment of his previous self.

"As you always have, Lord Lyran," the warrior said with a grin. "I should have known you'd survive."

Lyran nodded with a subtle glance at Ceph, lips tight, saying nothing.

"How many are you?" Dawn asked.

"There are seventeen of us." The warrior's tone turned somber. "As far as we know we're the only survivors of the battle. We made it out after the fighting and tried to follow the refugees, but... never caught up to them. Once we hit these open lands, we sought a place to hide for a while, to regain our strength."

Seventeen, of what had been an army of hundreds; a crushing blow.

We stayed with these soldiers, sharing a meager meal with them, food was scarce in these lands.

Falcon and Swift returned to us as the day turned to evening.

"There is a larger group a few valleys over," Swift said. "A good chunk of the refugees with some Njorva-soturi to protect them.

That was good news, but few in our group seemed to have their moods lifted by it. Roo did, and she tried to instill that hope in us, but... for some it didn't take: Ceph being the worst.

The next day we searched out this other group, following Swift's instructions on how to get to them, while Swift and Falcon kept searching for more. This new group was sizable indeed, nearly eight hundred refugees with a guard of thirty Njorvasoturi with ten Karhukora.

Iko and Eiva were also with this group, as was Iko's Uncle Mauno, who commanded this group of Njorva-soturi. He told us what he knew of what happened that fateful night. The line of refugees had been attacked by the eastern flank of the dragon lord's army. The Njor-vasoturi had repulsed them, again and again, fighting fearsomely, even with the restriction of the forest around them. They'd defeated the dragon lord's men, but many of the Njorvasoturi had died. Later, once they'd reached the edge of the forest, he'd separated off from Astraed. Each group had taken half of the remaining Njorvasoturi and roughly half of the refugees. Figuring two smaller groups would travel faster and hide easier. So, there were hopes we'd find that another group soon as well. Our spirits began to lift.

This group had found a large cave, well hidden in a craggy valley, also near a stream. It may have actually been the same watercourse we'd camped at the previous night, having travelled through rocks and hills to get here, but there was no way to know that for certain.

That night, I practiced fighting with Rhino, Lyran, and Mauno. Iko, Eiva, and several refugees were learning, though there weren't enough weapons to go around for all of them. Most of them had rough wooden staves. We tried to convince Ceph to fight, but he sat like a lump and just kept shaking his head. Dawn joined us as well.

First, we watched Lyran and Mauno spar. They were a sight indeed. Both strong and fast and experienced, an even match. Lyran was younger and had gifts from his dragon-bond, but Mauno was far more experienced and incredibly strong himself, his thick muscles knowing exactly how to move and react. Then we separated into two groups with Lyran instructing one, while Mauno led the other. Dawn and I were with Mauno. Iko, Eiva, and Rhino with Lyran.

I squared off with Mauno so he could test my level of ability. He was a massive mountain of a man, not as tall as Rhino, but with an impressive bulk of muscle on him. His testing strike against my wooden weapon easily knocked it down and away and he lifted his practice blade to strike at my arm. I spun in toward him and whipped my 'sword' around to tap his calf, as his 'sword' tapped my back.

"You're dead," Mauno said after we'd stepped back from the fight. "You've injured me, I'd have a lame leg, but I'd live. Why did you sacrifice yourself for a hit of little value?"

I grinned at him. "I didn't sacrifice myself. I'm tougher than I look." I was tiny for a man, especially amongst this group, and used to being underestimated. "Go ahead, hit me," I said, turning my back on him again. "Hard enough that you think you'd leave a bruise or knock me down." Since we weren't using bladed weapons, I wasn't too worried about cuts.

"You're mad," Mauno said.

"Maybe." I shrugged, nonchalant. "Try it," I urged him on.

Are you sure about this? Eona asked. *I know your avatar grants you a tougher hide, but Mauno is very strong.*

I have a feeling I'll be well, just wait and see.

Because of what happened with Eophon?

Exactly.

Mauno shrugged and slapped his wooden practice sword down on my back. I felt it... but more like a friend playfully punching you in the shoulder, not hard, but noticeable.

I laughed. "You can hit harder than that," I said.

"No, I can't," Mauno said, a bit of something odd in his voice. I turned to see he'd broken his practice sword. "This was made of steelwood, a root from the north, nearly unbreakable."

"Oh... ah, sorry," I apologized.

I guess we are tougher now, Eona said in awe. *Amazing!*

"Did you feel that at all?" Mauno asked, confused.

"Yeah, I felt it, but it didn't hurt."

"You are indeed tough. But... how does that hide of yours fare against steel itself?"

That was the question. Swan's dagger had pierced me, swords had cut me, if not deeply. But... I suspected things would be different now after my work with Eophon. I was curious just how different.

"Try your knife on me," I said to Mauno. "Here, on my side." There weren't any vital organs there and with Ceph's power still within me, I could heal it well enough.

"Now I know you're mad," Mauno said.

"Trust me," I said. "In addition to being tough, I can

also heal myself." To demonstrate I took out my own knife and stabbed it into my palm. Nothing happened, I hadn't broken skin. I tried harder and harder, but nothing. "Oh... well, trust me, I can heal myself."

Mauno shook his head. "It's your funeral." He took out his knife as I leaned over a bit, pulling up my shirt, exposing my side to him. His knife was made for slashing and he drew in a long breath then, holding the knife in a reversed grip, slashed along my side. The bladed skidded along my skin, not even leaving a mark.

"Harder," I urged him. That first hit had been a bit tentative.

He blinked, then shrugged and tried again. I felt the push of his strength against me and it almost knocked me over... but still the knife only barely cut me, not breaking skin.

"Try this one," I said, handing him my knife, a long stabbing blade.

He took it and looked at it for a long moment, then looked at my side, then my face, and back to the knife. He shook his head and slammed the knife into my side. It should have pierced well into me, but instead there was only a minor cut, perhaps a half-inch deep, then the blade bent.

I nodded. As I'd suspected.

Some part of what I'd done to Eophon, strengthening the dragon, had occurred in me as well. My skin was like steel now.

Truly amazing, Eona breathed.

It wouldn't have been possible without you and the spirit-gift you blessed me with, not to mention the harder hide to begin with.

Still!

Yeah, I know.

Mauno just kept shaking his head. "For one so small, you are... very tough indeed. I'd heard legends of some of my ancestors who shook off blade strikes like they were nothing, but until now I thought those tales only myths. Now I see... it is possible in some."

"I knew you were tough, but not like that." Rhino said, awed.

Perhaps now was the time to explain things. I told everyone of how I'd healed Eophon, making them stronger and tougher, reinforced with minerals from the earth, and how being a conduit had somehow done the same to me. The result of some strange mix of two different types of mystical power.

As I suspected, most of them just blinked in awe. Ceph... however, wore a bitter expression and slunk away into the night. I sighed.

Should I go after him?

I don't think it would help, not now, Eona advised. *He's too far gone into his depression.*

She was right. I wanted to help him, but I couldn't,

not yet. But I swore if there was some way to return his gift to him, I'd find it.

After that, the sparring continued, and others joined in to learn as well. I was surprised at the size of the group, many of the refugees — a group of over a hundred — wished to learn to fight. Perhaps they had been fleeing in terror from enemies for too long and sought to find a way to defend themselves. I could understand that.

And so went our days. For the next two weeks or so, we moved through the hilly lands, from one encampment to another, which Falcon or Swift had found the previous day. And in the evenings, a growing group of people would train with weapons. As our numbers grew, we began to fashion some weapons for our new and growing army, though they were crude, since our only forge was Eophon's fire.

By the time we had scoured the bad-lands, we had found nearly all of the Oseran and Basian refugees, sixteen-hundred men and women. We'd also gathered many small pockets of men from Lyran's army which had survived the battle or had been escorting refugees, roughly two hundred men. And finally, there were a little over sixty Njorvasoturi with twenty Karhukora. Adding to our fighting force were nearly three-hundred refugees, learning to fight with various weapons.

The first true village we came to, was Dwa Brody in

the northeast of Basia. The dragon lord's men hadn't occupied it yet, since it was small and out of the way. But the village had heard rumors of an advancing army of a hundred-thousand men. Spirits fell once more. Few believed our small force could stop the Thraian Horde.

Lyran believed the battle in the forest had only been a small fraction of the dragon lord's men, perhaps five thousand. We'd faced five-to-one odds and bled them deeply, but had paid a significant price ourselves. This time, they outnumbered us two hundred to one.

It was impossible.

CHAPTER 10

ROO

DWA BRODY WAS A QUIET, LAKE-SIDE VILLAGE AND welcomed all of us. The war hadn't reached them, yet. Though with the recent news many were thinking of fleeing east.

Dwa Brody meant 'two fords,' since the village sat on a north-south road which passed over a river on both sides of town. The small town sat on a hill, picturesque and pleasant. Docks stretched out into the lake at the bottom of the hill on the eastern side. To the west were farmlands, flanked by a set of low hills to the north, and a small forest to the south.

The more Lyran and Dawn looked at this town, the more they loved its strategic value. There was a lot they could do to make a battle here unfavorable for an attacking force. So, they got to work doing that. At the same time Falcon and Swift scouted deeper into Basia to see if they could find the approaching Thraian forces. It didn't take them long. The army was on the move, heading east to Elista.

A small group of us met in the common room of Dwa Brody's one tavern to discuss what we would do.

"There are too many of them," Astraed said firmly. "If we fight here, we die. Better to fall back to Elista and aid Dawn's mother's forces."

"We can make this village work for us, I know it. I'm already planning it. Just..." Lyran grimaced. He'd tried to talk field strategy to Astraed and Mauno, but they were warriors who'd only ever known small skirmishes and intimate tactical battles. Fighting a force like the Thraians out in the open seemed impossible to them. Hardened warriors as they were, they still couldn't see the apparent advantages of this place. Lyran went over it again.

"We take out the fords so they can't flank us. The only way to do so would be to make boats, which would take time, and I know they won't do it. They'll think this an easy defeat.

"And it isn't?" Mauno asked, skeptical.

"No. Once we take out the fords, they'll have to come at us from the west. Yes, they'll destroy the farms there, but it will be a small price to pay if we stop the Thraians here and now. They'll be funneled tight, by that hill to the north and the forest to the south.

They'll not be able to come at us in a massive long line, nor surround us. At best they could get a hundred men abreast, two hundred if they're packed tight. Which means our archers on the hill here—" He pointed to a spot at the edge of the village on the rough map he'd drawn. "—will be able to just fire and forget, they'll almost certainly hit something as long as there isn't a strong cross-wind."

"And won't they just march up that hill and kill our archers?" Astraed asked.

"What they'd probably do is send their cavalry at them. But even so, they won't be able to come from a flank. They'll be at the head of the army, riding straight into the archers, and... if we make this area here—" This time he stabbed his finger down at a swath of land between the two rivers at the base of the hill the village sat upon. "—into a swamp by cutting deep canals through it so the river-water rushes in... then their cavalry will be stopped dead. They'll struggle through the swamp, giving our archers more time to cut them down. And the wonderful part is their infantry will have to march through that swamp as well. It will tire them out and slow them down. And when, eventually they finally get to the other side of the swamp and start up the hill... That's when your beasts will charge out of hiding on either side of the village and crush them in repeated charges across their numbers."

"What of their archers?" Mauno asked. "If they set

up archers on this hill here, or on either side of the fords they can rain down death upon us."

"True, but that's where Eophon will help us, strafing their men with fire."

"And won't their dragon be hindering yours?" Astraed asked. "That... didn't go well for you last time." She grimaced. "And what if the other dragon does defeat yours, or what if it ignores yours and just decides to burn this village with all of us in it?"

Lyran's jaw clenched for a long moment. "We have a plan for that too. Plus, Eophon is stronger now." None of us really understood what Pan had done, but we couldn't deny Eophon's own assertions of his improved durability and prowess.

"We have only your word on that," Astraed said.

"And mine," Pan piped up.

"Look, the plan is solid." Lyran was trying to keep his cool. I sent him a few waves of calm, and after a long breath he began again. "Our plan is solid. I'll be on that hill outside the town, no dragon visible, looking like I'm all alone. My brother could destroy me, but I'm willing to bet he wants to fight me himself. He'll land and get off Thavralian to fight me one-on-one. He knows he has the advantage in such combat, and he'll want to show me, but I'll have Pan and Midnight there with me to help me defeat him. And Eophon will be waiting close by to deal with Thavralian. All he needs to do is take out one of the other dragon's wings. Once he does, Thavralian will be grounded, virtually helpless. Eophon will tear him apart, then deal with those archers, if they even bother with archers. I still think they'll just come straight at us, trusting their numbers to destroy us."

"And won't they?" Mauno sounded tired, already a little defeated. "You've said they have a hundred thousand men. We have barely six hundred and most of those are raw, new warriors. Even if all the other elements of your plan work, even if we can cut them down to half, or even eliminate ninety percent of their forces, which I think is unlikely, they'll still have ten thousand men to our six hundred and that's assuming we haven't taken any casualties in all that fighting. It's..." The large man sighed. "I don't like to use the word, but impossible certainly seems like what we're facing now."

Lyran rubbed a hand over his face. It was late. "I have to hope it will work."

"I... may have a way for us to help even the odds," Dawn said sounding curious even at her own suggestion.

I however, had had enough of this. I wasn't one who knew anything about war and I'd been invited as a courtesy, but I excused myself then. Half of them didn't even notice I left as they continued their discussion.

The night air was cool and refreshing when I

stepped outside. I drank it in with several long breaths.

"Roo?" The voice was almost not recognizable. Almost, but I knew who it was.

"Ceph?" I turned. He sat outside the tavern on the ground looking up at the stars. "What is it?"

"I think... I'm ready to talk."

I nodded. It was a testament to how weak he'd become that I had to help him up, offering a hand. He leaned on me as we walked a little way, out of the village to the hillside overlooking the lake. There we sat and I waited for him, sending him reassurance and hope, though as usual, it felt like everything I sent him was devoured into the void of his soul.

"I'm sorry," he began, and as soon as he said it, he began weeping softly. "I failed you," he whispered through his tears.

I put an arm around him, pulling him close. He'd always been a lean man, but the meagre rations and his own refusal to eat these past weeks meant he felt thin and frail now, hardly there. I held him and waited for him to speak again, as I made soft noises of reassurance and whispered, "I love you."

He drew in a shuddering breath. "I... I had to save Lyran. He was dying."

"I know," I whispered. "Thank you."

"But... but I couldn't!" he cried out. "I didn't have enough in me."

"But you did, he's still alive..."

"But it cost me too much," he said bitterly. "It cost me everything."

I wondered at this, but said nothing, waiting for him to go on. When he hadn't after a long while I prompted with: "Tell me everything, Ceph."

I felt him nod, head on my shoulder. He spoke haltingly. "I couldn't heal him. My gift... it wasn't meant for healing. I can only move healthy bits around and disperse the wounded bits so they're not a worry. It wasn't meant... and... and Lyran didn't have enough healthy parts of him left. He was utterly broken and dying. I... I couldn't use his own tissue to save him, so... I used mine."

Oh! I worked very hard not to say that out loud. I knew roughly how Ceph's gift worked, able to adjust a person physically to do many things, disguise them, make them tougher, but as he said, it wasn't meant for healing. Still, I hadn't known he could exchange parts of his own body for another's.

It explains a lot, Leoa said. *He literally lost himself, a part of himself.*

How horrible, and yet... such love for Lyran.

I suspect, as much as he loved the other man, his love was mostly for you. Knowing you'd feel Lyran's loss deeply.

Ah, yes, you're probably right.

Ceph went on: "I tore at myself and I gave everything, and when I could take no more from me, I tore at my gift itself. I gave... *everything* to Lyran, so he could live. And I was left... broken. I... gave too much of myself. I... I lost my gift and... it feels like I'm not... all here anymore. I'm half a man and the other half is in Lyran."

Spirits, that was awful! "Oh, Ceph, I'm so sorry." I rubbed his arm gently.

"I saved him, but I... I emptied myself to do it." He began weeping softly again. "And... and when I think back on it, I know... I know it was the right thing to do. I'm nothing, but he's a prince, a dragon lord, he needs to be there to defeat his brothers and reform Thraan. I'm... nothing. I was never important and now I'm truly nothing." He broke down, sobbing.

Ah, so there is more to this than just his physical loss.

I never knew he had such deep-seated insecurities, I said. *He'd always seemed so sure and strong.*

He may have been, perhaps hiding his fears until he had no physical or emotional fortitude to quell them.

Perhaps.

I turned to him, holding him close to my breast, and he soaked the front of my dress in tears.

"No Ceph, you are important, to me, to Dawn and her mother. You are a brave and loving Noble of the nation of Elista, and you've helped us through so much. It took great courage and sacrifice to do what you did. Never think you're nothing, you're an amazing man, so giving and loving."

He wept more but said nothing.

Now I understood. And I think I even knew why my emotional transference wasn't working. He may have lost more than just some of his body. He may have even lost part of his soul, his very spirit itself. And if he had no hope — not just an absence of hope, but if his soul didn't even know what hope was anymore — then how could I try to instill it?

Blessed Spirits! How horrible.

"I swear, Ceph, I'll find a way to fix this. I don't know how, yet, but I will. You've done far too much for me, been there in my darkest moments, when I feared for my life and my soul. So I swear, I'll be there for you and find some way to undo this. What's done can be undone. If we can bring men back from the brink of death, we can restore their bodies and souls from the brink of collapse. I know it, and I will not stop until I find a way to mend this for you."

He sniffed and pulled back to look up at me. "How?" was all he said.

I smiled at him. "Leave the how to me, for now, you just know it *will* happen. That is a promise I intend to keep."

He blinked and in those clear blue eyes, I saw his soul laid bare, broken and shredded, but with just the faintest glimmer of hope. I was overjoyed to see that even that sliver of optimism remained. His lips trembled and he wept freely again, head upon my breast, though I sensed a difference in this outflow of tears.

This time... he was weeping with the belief that his pain might end.

And I held him all the closer, knowing I had to end it.

I would need to talk to Dawn, she was stronger in spirit that I was, but that would be where I'd begin.

The trouble was... Dawn was incredibly busy over the next few days. She and Lyran were putting their plan into motion and the countryside around Dwa Brody was being transformed. No one had any free time, even I was conscripted into helping make arrows, learning how to smooth shafts with sandstone or fish scales, before handing them off to true fletchers who did the more delicate work with feathers.

We all did our part. And a few brave souls even sacrificed themselves well before the fight began. We needed Aaghar's army to know we were here, to come to us. So, a few civilians, unable to fight and with no family left to live for, volunteered to ride south and west. To find the dragon lord's army and ensure they knew Dawn and I were here. They'd say they were trying to flee back to their homes, to avoid the war, and when 'questioned' they would 'give up' our location.

Once Swan knew we were here, she'd come, and she'd hopefully bring the full might of Aaghar's army with her.

Those stalwart souls would be the first casualties of this battle, and I wasn't so naïve as to think they would be the last. Where there was battle there was death, and this battle would be our most challenging yet.

CHAPTER 11

DAWN

WE HAD A PLAN FOR EVERYTHING; EVERYTHING EXCEPT... how to deal with Swan. She was a wildcard and far too powerful. She could easily ruin our plans, which meant, I needed to know how to defeat her when I next met her.

Not that I had any free time to think about it. My days were filled with hours upon hours of hard work, and my nights — short as they were — were spent in exhausted sleep. I worked on the canals between the two rivers, which would create a swamp the enemy would have to cross. That meant hours of digging trenches. It was hard and inglorious work, but necessary. The second most important work being done was making the thousands of arrows our archers would need to have a hope of whittling down the enemy. Smiths, including Pan, worked in forges day and night, crafting swords and arrowheads. Carpenters created a long, covered area on the side of the hill, to protect our archers from incoming enemy arrows. Still others worked on destroying the two fords at the rivers so we'd not be flanked by enemy forces. And the hours we weren't working or sleeping, usually morning and evening, were spent in combat practice, training everyone who wished to learn.

In truth, the residents of Dwa Brody were not entirely happy we'd taken over their town, destroying their farms, and bringing doom upon their quiet village. Many fled into the surrounding hills. Most of our civilians went with them. We made sure they were well provisioned. Those who knew this fight was necessary stayed and helped as they could. The town had a militia of thirty or so men, with three who had once been members of the royal army. It wasn't much of an addition to our forces, but we would take any help we could get.

Falcon reported on the enemy's movements. Our sacrificial informants had done their job. The massive army had turned north. They'd be here in a week, since an army of that size didn't move quickly.

We completed the impromptu swamp two days before the army arrived. All the other preparations were coming along as well. Everyone who could, helped make arrows those last two days, and with that effort we were able to create fifty thousand arrows. It wasn't nearly enough, but it would have to do. With the — fingers crossed, I hoped he came through — surprise Swift was obtaining for me... we *might possibly* win this fight, but it was still an incredible long-shot.

And that night, still a day and a bit before the enemy was to arrive, a small council of us gathered to finally talk about Swan.

"I can't reach her with my emotional push," Roo said, shaking her head. "I won't be of much use against her." She sighed. "Plus, I'll have my hands full with the rest of the army."

I nodded. Since Roo wasn't a warrior, she'd be doing her best to filter despair and hopelessness into the enemy ranks. That alone would be a monumental task for an army that size.

"And with all my strength, from what I have been told, even I wouldn't be able to break past this shield around her," Rhino said. He was still a little uncertain and unsettled. Lyran had had a long talk with the man, trying to explain that going one-on-one with Aaghar was a near-death-sentence and Rhino was lucky to have done what he did and survived. Still the large man was... hesitant.

"And those bolts of energy Swan shoots, they could quickly destroy our lines," Falcon added.

I knew all of this. "I need answers, not doubts and questions." I sighed. "Each of you, ask your Lumani, what is known about spirit gifts, can they be... stopped or weakened or... something?"

Well, I asked Amya. *Any thoughts?*

You are only the second Bonded I've had who's had a spirit gift. The truth is that they are a mystery to human and Lumani alike. We don't know how they occur, nor why they only appear in some True-Bonded and not others. Until now, we simply accepted they were gifts. No one's put any true thought into how to foil them.

"There is one option..." Pan said slowly. "Though I do not like it."

I grimaced, thinking I knew what he was thinking. "You could try to borrow her powers and fight her one on one?"

He nodded.

"No. First, we need you with Lyran and Midnight fighting Aaghar. Second, we need your healing gift. After all this is done, no matter who wins, there will be far too many people who need healing. We can't risk you losing that gift for the possibility you could take Swan. We need another way."

He shrugged nodding.

What about our gift? Amya asked me. *We can sense the subtlest shifts in the air, in a person's movements. We can feel and see the connections between all things. So, perhaps... perhaps we can use that to connect with a spirit gift as well?*

I had never considered that. *Do you think that's even possible?*

I have no clue, but we can try to find out.

Yes, we could. We had several people here with gifts on whom we could experiment. But I'd keep that as a backup option for now. Yet, the others had no thoughts either. Their Lumanis' reactions were similar to Amya: *we've always accepted them, and don't know where they come from, no one's ever tried to get rid of one.*

Which left Amya's long-shot option.

"I... may have a way to do it?" I said, purposefully sounding unsure. "Tomorrow I'll want to borrow all of you to test my theory."

"What are you going to do?" Pan asked.

I grinned. "I'm going to try to connect with your spirit-gifts... then... I'm going to try to take them." That got a few gasps and surprised looks. I smiled at them. "Don't worry, it's all theory right now. Mostly I want to see if connecting with a spirit gift is even possible."

So, the next day a few of us gathered on the lake-ward, side of the town. It was a warm fall day, the trees in the forest on the other side of the hill were starting to show colors, but alas too many of us had far more on our minds than the beauty of nature. The army would arrive tomorrow.

Falcon, Rhino, Pan, and Lyran had come with Roo and me. Ceph hadn't been up for anything, and Swift was still off on my 'secret mission.'

I began with Roo. "Your ability allows you to connect with what others are feeling and push emotions into them. That is something I can feel. So, let's start there. Send me a little bit of your love," I said.

She smiled and obliged. I felt the warmth of her love seep into me. I felt it mid-chest just below and between my breasts and it made me smile. "Good, keep that up."

I closed my eyes and, drawing a deep breath, simply let my own gift seep out of me. I felt those around me, their presences, their power. I felt the fish, teaming in the lake, and the birds above me. The wind upon my skin whispered of its power, how it moved and eddied and swirled around all of us. Then I focused inward to that spot of deepest love I could feel within me.

At first, I could feel only my own inner workings: the beat of my heart, the swell and contraction of my lungs, the burbling of my stomach. I felt the strength of my ribs and the flow of my blood, but nothing beyond the physical.

So, I tried something different, keeping part of my focus on that spot in my chest, I also reached out to Roo and sent my spirit-senses over her, seeing if I could find the connection between us.

Almost immediately I sensed something, and it was so surprising it bumped me out of my calm state and my concentration lapsed.

"Oh!" I gasped opening my eyes wide.

"What?" Roo asked. "Did you feel it? Did you sense my spirit-gift?"

"No," I said slowly. "I sensed something else entirely." Perhaps it was the love still warm in my chest or my shock, but I went to Roo and hugged her fiercely. "I love you, my dearest, closest, most wonderful friend, my sister-in-spirit."

She embraced me slowly, perhaps a bit stunned. "I love you too, Dawn. What... did you feel?"

"I felt... us," I said, not knowing truly how to express it. "I felt our connection, Roo. I don't know if it's our shared avatar or... or even more, but... I felt the connection between us. Something deep, something of pure spirit. I... I'd always known we were connected, but... this is the first time I fully felt it... and it was a wonderful and amazing thing!"

Roo laughed lightly, perhaps sensing my own giddiness. "Do you think that will help you do what you need to do?" she asked.

It might.

I stood on my toes and pulled her down to kiss her cheek. "Perhaps, let me try again." There were tears in both of our eyes at the overwhelming love and sisterhood we'd shared in that moment. And as I closed my moistened eyes, I found that connection again easily. It was like... like a slender tendril of spirit which connected us inexorably, so fragile but still stronger than steel.

I sent some of my gift through that connection and... a whole other world blossomed before me. I was in Roo's spirit and it was... stunning.

I fell to my knees, weeping freely.

"Dawn, what's wrong?" Roo asked.

"Nothing... you're just so... beautiful... on the inside."

Like the time Lyran had been within my soul and we'd been beings of pure spirit — our true colors — so I was within Roo now. She was everything that was spring and life and love. Yellow, pink, and rose, upon a rich bed of verdant green, like a field of flowers. There were pale blues, like a spring sky, and the fiery hot white, which seemed a common threat among most of us. I recalled my own colors, the hues of power: burning reds and oranges, with sun-light yellow and pure white. Roo was softer, the colors of love and life and I had been truly overwhelmed with the sense of belonging and peace I felt within her.

I pulled out from her spirit, regaining myself slowly, smiling at this precious gift I'd been given. As I did, I used my gift again, sensing along the connection between us, but other than the resonance of that bond, I didn't feel anything which seemed like her gift. So, I drew back again. I focused on myself, and that still-warm spot of love in my chest, then focused on Roo, not her physical form, not even her spirit in truth. Just... seeking for something which seemed like it connected with this spot I felt.

I caressed the curves of her spirit and felt its power. And something, some small niggling feeling began to grow in me.

I stilled myself and concentrated on this new feeling. I left off trying to connect and just... let myself be connected to Roo.

And there it was.

I felt more than just our connection, which I think had been partially blinding me before. I felt something else, another connection, like an ethereal tether from her to me, from her heart to my heart. It was warm, like the feeling in my chest.

"Change the emotion you're sending, something substantially different than love," I asked.

"I... I don't want to send you anything negative," Roo said softly. "Here's... a sense of awe."

I felt the warmth fade, replaced by an expansive sense of wonder.

"Oh! Yes!" Not only did that make me feel good, but I'd isolated where I was sensing that and what it felt like.

Now for the tricky part. "Now move your gift to someone else."

I felt the expansive feeling fade. "Done."

I drew in a long breath and reached out with this

new deeper sense of connection. I felt for Roo first, it was her power I was trying to sense. And like before, feeling around her spirit, I found a spot, an ethereal tether reaching out from her to another.

I imagined my spirit sense was a blade and I slashed through that tether.

"Oh!" I heard the combined gasps of Roo and Lyran. "Was that you? It felt..."

"Sorry," I said opening my eyes. "I had to see if I could interact with your gift while it was being used. I guess I did."

"So that *was* you?" Lyran asked. "You can sever a person's gift?"

"I don't know if I can stop the gift entirely, but I was able to stop it from being used. I need some more practice, to see what else is possible." We all rejoiced at that, but there was still a lot of work to do.

I spent the rest of the morning connecting to each of their spirit-gifts, feeling the differences and the subtleties. Roo's was easy to sense because it reached out from her. Falcon's was also easy since it was a connection between him and his brother, who was not with us at the moment. I felt the long tendril snaking out from him to Swift. Pan's was particularly difficult to feel, since it was two gifts in one. Yet, with work, I was able to sense his true gift to borrow other's gifts.

I didn't want to actually remove any of their gifts, but we played around with what I could do for the rest of the morning, strengthening this new aspect to my own gift. I just hoped it would be enough to stop Swan.

And after we'd eaten a picnic on the hillside to refresh ourselves... laughing and finally feeling like perhaps we'd have a chance against this impossible force coming against us... we all felt a rather over-whelming need to join physically. And so began a rather naughty afternoon of incredible pleasure.

CHAPTER 12

ROO

NONE OF US KNEW WHAT WOULD HAPPEN TOMORROW. As much as we'd planned and prepared, death was a very real option. That made our lovemaking that afternoon all the more intense and immediate.

Lyran's tongue slid over my folds, adding moisture which wasn't needed as I yearned for him to finally be inside me. But he was determined to take his time, as was Falcon, who lay beside me, his lips upon mine, his hands softly caressing my breasts. His cock was in just the right spot for my hand to stroke, slowly moving over the rigid flesh.

Beside me, Dawn was being pleasured by Rhino and Pan, but I paid little attention to them, focusing on my own two wonderful men.

Lyran clamped his mouth over me, softly sucking

my clitoris. And when he flicked his tongue over it, I found my first orgasm as a surprising spike of pleasure shot through me. I sighed out a long moan as my body tensed. Falcon's nimble fingers, deftly circling and plucking at my nipples help to draw out the peak of that first release as the intensity of his kisses promised more passion to come.

Lyran lifted away from me, kneeling, shifting in as his hands opened my legs to accommodate him, massaging my inner thighs. I felt the heaviness of his long cock come to rest upon my folds. Then he slowly shifted back and forth, running this entire length over me in mock thrusts. He knew he'd not be able to fit fully inside me, but I imagined he was picturing his fullness pushing into me, pressing to the hilt. Perhaps, if Pan joined us later, he'd be able to do just that, but for now, this seemed to satisfy him. He shifted, the heavy tip of his cock now pressing down on me. He pushed into me slowly, then paused, letting out a heavy, shuddering sigh.

"Soft or hard," he asked.

"Soft for now," I said trembling as my passion built yet again. "Hard later."

"Yes, M'lady," he said, and began a slow and gentle push deeper inside me. He rocked through several long thrusts, inching a bit farther each time until I felt him press upon my utmost depths. My back arched as a heavy wave of pleasure rippled through me.

I moaned into Falcon's mouth, and needing him closer, wrapped my arms around his neck, kissing deeper. And when his lips slid off mine, they came to whisper hot breath in my ear. "My goddess is truly divine. How shall I worship thee?"

"Make me come," I whispered back. "I think a dozen orgasms are enough for a goddess." I gave a breathy, half-laugh-half gasp.

You're a greedy little goddess, aren't you? Leoa purred inside me. *But I won't complain.*

"As you wish," Falcon said and moved his kisses down to my breasts, using lips, teeth and tongue to cover my fullness with his moisture. His hand traced down over my belly to stroke my clitoris as Lyran moved inside me. Then Falcon's hand shifted off me, and I heard Lyran grunt. Falcon's hand pushed again and again on my folds around Lyran's cock, and I assumed he was stroking the other man.

Lyran trembled inside me, swelling, but then he seemed to stiffen even more as he grunted. "Not. Yet." Was he controlling his own release? Spirits, the man was amazing! He pushed fully into me and stayed there, pressing hard against that point of deep pleasure and ratcheting up my bliss from soft hills to jagged mountains.

"Yes," I breathed, back arching again, pressing my breasts up into Falcon's lips. He plucked up and sucked a ragingly hard nipple, his teeth raking the ultra-sensitive nub. His hand upon Lyran returned to rub my clitoris savagely. That, along with Lyran's deep push, made me cry out as I hit a hard, body-contracting release. I writhed and lost myself in the bliss of the moment before that wave passed and found I was only racing higher and higher into my ecstasy.

I wanted control... now.

I pushed Falcon off me and sat up, putting my arms around Lyran's neck for support as I rocked myself on his cock. His face was tight, tense, teeth gritted.

"Come," I whispered to him, knowing he'd been holding back.

"Not yet," he gasped. And that was one of the reasons why I loved him.

He lifted me, hands under my round bottom as I wrapped my legs around him. Then he shifted, slowly laying himself back so I could truly take control and straddle him.

I kept the pressure on, heavy upon his cock, feeling him pressing so deep inside me. Then as Falcon had done, I grasped the extra few inches of his cock outside of me and stroked him. This time I smiled with pure mischief as I repeated what I'd said earlier. "Come," I breathed. He just smiled, still trembling and tense, shaking his head.

That man has amazing restraint! Leoa gasped as our bliss spiked. *I could just eat him up!*

That's when I felt the cold touch of slickness upon my other opening. Falcon was oiling me. But I was already well aroused, and my puckered rear entrance opened at his touch. He quickly had two fingers inside me, massaging more oil around as I felt a massive wave of passion build, starting in my toes and slowly filling me with tingling bliss.

When Falcon filled me with his cock, plunging deep, I let out a very unladylike sound of grunting pleasure. Those two throbbing erections pressed close inside me made molten heat bubble in my core. I bounced hard — I hoped not too hard — on Lyran's stiff cock as Falcon grabbed my hips and began a vicious thrusting from behind. The heat of my passion consumed me, climbing up from my hips to my breasts and my face. I continued that heavy, loud groaning, sweat glistening upon me. I was so near, so ready, so close to an explosion of ecstasy. Then Lyran's hands came up and engulfed my heavy breasts, gripping hard, pressing and caressing, and I was thrown over the edge, into a yawning chasm of radiant bliss.

I felt like I became a being of pure light, exploding with energy and love, pulsing with pounding ecstasy as I came, over and over. With each thrust of Falcon, and each press of Lyran upon my deepest point, I exploded again and again. Then I heard Lyran's vicious, feral cry and felt his own blast of warmth inside me, powerful and pure. His hands upon my breast clenched painfully tight, but that spike of pain only seemed to add to the transcendent joy of that moment.

And when Falcon's final thrust and powerful release hit me... I found a new height to my bliss. I was a cloud, warm and high and floating with careless joy through the ether; billowing and peaceful on top, but with a raging storm below, torrential rains pouring out of me while flashes of tingling lightning shot to all my extremities.

When I finally came to myself again, I was bathed in sweat and the three of us were lying on our sides together, still pressed close.

"That was amazing," I whispered.

Best Orgasm Ever! Leoa shouted inside me.

"We know," Lyran said with a chuckle.

"You let us know," Falcon added. "You made us feel it too. My body is still tingling."

I giggled, which caused me to clamp a little tighter on both of their cocks still inside me. They both gasped then laughed. "Just wait," I whispered. "I'm going to get you to rouse me again, then share that with you so you're ready for round two."

"I think I'm ready now," Lyran whispered, then kissed my lips softly.

Spirits!

"Yeah, me too." Falcon kissed my neck and shoulders from behind.

Best men ever! Leoa shouted, and I had to agree.

I felt truly peaceful and joyful in that moment and was quickly growing heated with their renewed passion.

CHAPTER 13

DAWN

I HADN'T BEEN WITH RHINO SINCE THAT NIGHT I'D turned him away in the forest. He'd apologized after talking with Roo, but we just hadn't had the time nor the privacy to be together in the days that had followed. He was still processing some things but was far different now than he had been then; far more willing to accommodate me.

Are you going to ask him to shrink his cock like you did before? Amya inquired.

I don't know, maybe, we'll see what I want... Maybe I want his full cock, even if he can't get it all in.

What about what he wants?

Oh, that's important too, but this is his chance to show me he's willing to be with me on even terms, not demanding.

Ah.

I helped Rhino apply oil to his massive cock as we

knelt together. Pan was behind me, kissing my back and shoulders, his hands around me, softly kneading my breasts as I worked to make Rhino... so very wet.

"I will do anything you wish," Rhino said softly, gasping at my two-handed attention to oiling his cock. "Tell me, and I shall comply."

It seems he's come around, Amya said.

And I'm very happy he has. And hopefully I'll be coming around him soon enough.

Dirty girl.

And you love it!

Yeah, you're right.

I laid myself back. Pan moved from behind me to beside. I put my hands under my ass and lifted it, opening my legs. "I got you wet, now it's your turn."

Rhino smiled. "More than happy to oblige," he whispered as he pressed thick fingers upon my folds.

Turning my head to Pan. "I want your cock," I said, then curled my tongue to let him know where. He shifted closer, lowering himself next to my head. I took his cock in one hand and brought it to my lips, getting him very wet as well.

Rhino pressed and probed, delving inside me with one finger while his thumb flashed over my clit. I moaned around Pan's cock as I felt my pussy grow wet. Rhino removed his one finger, to plunge another into me, covering it in my juices before he added that first finger back. I nearly came when those two fingers plunged into me. I was small after all, and his fingers were thick and long. Then he lifted his thumb away to press the base of his palm over my clit. The two fingers inside me curled up, and he shifted back and forth over those two stimulating points.

As Rhino rocked harder and faster with his hand, Pan reached down to grasp one of my small breasts, massaging it. Bringing his fingers together, he gently pressed upon a hard and pointed nipple. That did it.

I came so hard I had to take a break from Pan's cock to scream my appreciation. I soaked Rhino's hand as my pussy overflowed with my release. With my hips raised as they were, I felt moisture run rivulets down my belly and over my ass.

"Put that big cock inside me!" I gasped. "I want you, now!" I had to be ready for him after that!

"As you wish, mistress," Rhino said, removing his fingers to position the massive head of his cock at my opening.

"Do you want me to—" Pan began.

"No," I cut off Pan. I didn't want him to adjust either of us yet. I wanted to feel Rhino's full cock with my own tiny pussy. I wanted to feel the pull and pressure as he forced me wider and wider, filling me as I was...

"Are you sure?" Rhino asked. "You're wet, but..."

"Force it in," I growled. "Now." I stared him down and he nodded.

I was panting, desperate for that massive cock. Next

to me, Pan gasped, and I realized my hand around his cock had been squeezing tight. I put him back in my mouth as Rhino began his push.

I had felt so open, so loose around his magical fingers, but even so, I felt the heavy press of his cock upon me and still I wasn't big enough. But my last words had been clear, I didn't care if it hurt, I wanted him to assault my pussy until he fit.

Large, grasping hands engulfed my thighs, pulling me as Rhino grunted with his effort to penetrate me. I felt myself open a little more, it seemed almost enough, my folds had almost embraced his tip

"Eternal Lights!" Pan whispered. "It's too big, he can't fit!"

I squeezed Pan's cock again to draw his attention down to me shaking my head, with his cock still in my mouth. I didn't want him to interfere. I wanted to feel every aching moment of this. Rhino gave another hard push, but instead his cock slipped out entirely. His tip glistened with oil and my juices, looking glorious and huge above me.

"Enough," Rhino gasped, and grabbed his cock. He slid his hand down to the tip and I saw him squeeze it, hard, compressing it just a little. He grunted in pain as he repositioned it at my opening and pushed through the tight press of his hand into the tight press of my canal.

That seemed to work, as he finally entered me. He

made sure the tip was in plus a bit more, then grabbed my hips and grunted loudly as he thrusted deeper, fully into me. It felt like he was tearing me apart and I gasped around Pan's cock, nearly passing out with the intensity of pleasure and pain that crashed down upon me.

Rhino had been inside me once before without any adjustments to either of us, and that had been a body-shattering experience. He seemed even larger this time and my mind couldn't quite comprehend the massive fullness pressing so very deep inside me. More of his cock was outside of me, than in, but still he was utterly filling me.

I released Pan's cock long enough to give Rhino his next set of instructions. "Now thrust like you mean it!" I heard pain in my rasping voice, and so did Pan and Rhino.

"Dawn, he'll—"

"Tear me a new one? Yeah, that's the idea, you can heal it later," I said to Pan.

Rhino heard this and shook his head in shock. But then... that same feral intensity that had come over him before descended over his eyes and my body turned to jelly as I trembled in anticipation of what was to come.

His thrusts weren't long, or he'd slip out of me, but they were hard. He leaned over me, grabbing my hips to deliver powerful, shocking pulses of his massive erection pounding into me.

And with each, pummeling shock, I came. Each thrust only added to my pleasure, as I gasped and moaned, or cried out around Pan's cock. It was too much for Pan, and quickly his hot release filled my mouth. I jerked his cock with my hand, squeezing every last drop out of him as he groaned and called out as well.

And Rhino kept pounding away, breaking me.

Once Pan had finished, I released him, nearly delirious with this odd mix of painful pleasure surging through me over and over and over again, sending my ecstasy through the roof.

"Now," I gasped at Pan, and hoped he understood.

He nodded and cupped my breast with one hand. As he did, I felt an odd tingling inside me as I was changed. And now, each of Rhino's thrusts drove deeper and deeper still and the large man's grunts shifted up a notch, as he sensed that he could finally be fully inside me.

I couldn't support my up-lifted hips anymore, even with my own better-than-human strength. Rhino's bombardment was too much and when I collapsed under him, he adjusted quickly. He grabbed my legs by the ankles, pressing them forward and out. It was a good thing I was flexible as my knees pressed down beside my breasts with my feet above my head and his relentless cock driving into me so deep, I felt him in the same spot where I'd felt Roo's love earlier.

And Pan's light touch filled me with tingling bliss centralized around that massive cock, so that with each thrust I blossomed with orgasm after orgasm.

Then with a final hard thrust, and an animalistic roar, Rhino had his own body-shaking release. And having gone without for so long, it was powerful and lingering as he spread warmth through my chest, then seemingly to my entire body. I had no clue what Pan was doing, but it felt amazing, and I lay in the dazed aftermath of such powerful sex. My head spun, my eyes were unfocused, my body warm and constantly trembling with one long, drawn-out after-shock of ecstatic bliss from the dozens of orgasms I'd just experienced. I was so incredibly sensitive that when Pan leaned over and blew a breath over my skin, I was caught in the throes of yet another orgasm.

"Please!" I begged.

"Please stop or please continue?" Pan asked with a mischievous grin.

The trouble was, I didn't know which I wanted.

So, he kissed a nipple and I shuddered and came again.

"Keep that up and I'll come again too," Rhino said, gruff and hoarse. He wasn't even finished with his first release, still pulsing inside of me. But I realized I'd been clamping down on him with every one of my new after-orgasms.

"Yes, master," I said teasing.

Then the wind picked up a little and just the touch of that breeze upon me sent me into a series of tense thrills.

Pan laughed.

Rhino grunted and found his own set of after-shocks.

That was... so... barbaric and hard and... Amya was practically purring inside me.

Curious, knowing that Amya had had mostly male True-Bonded hosts before me, I asked: *How does it feel to be on the other end of such a powerful cock?*

I... I knew being with you would be different, Amya began, voice still shaking a little with bliss. *I never imagined anything like this, though. I wouldn't have thought that added spike of pain could be so thrilling. I can't imagine every woman would like it, but you... you... you...* Amya seemed lost for words.

Yeah, I'm amazing, I know.

You are. And I sensed Amya's sincerity.

"I need a break, for just a moment," I said to my two wonderful guys. Then, to Pan as Rhino slowly withdrew that monster cock: "And I'll take that healing now."

Rhino and Pan shifted. The large man lay beside me, and we kissed and played a little as Pan caressed me all over around my belly, hips, and thighs, returning me to normal and healing me.

After that, I simply lay in the sun for a while, the men on either side of me, kissing back and forth as they traced lines over my sensitive skin. I loved the warmth of the sun upon me and the coolness of the breeze off the lake as I slowly recovered.

Then Rhino left, though not before Pan had adjusted his cock to be a better fit for Roo, and I was joined by Lyran and Falcon. Pan stayed with me, of course. Roo would get some alone time with the massive Rhino while I got my group-love on.

I think with my next host I'd like to Bond with a man who sleeps with men. After being with you, I'm curious what that would be like, Amya mused.

I'm sure it will be wonderful, but nothing will compare to me, I said with playful vanity.

Amya laughed at that. *Yes, I know. You'll be very hard to replace. You're one of a kind, Dawn.*

That I am.

"You seem restful, what would you like?" Falcon asked. He had something in his hands, playing with it. I recognized the small toy Swift had used when we'd been up north.

"I don't care. I've already had more orgasms today than I can count. I'm happy, so do what you like."

Falcon grinned. "I was hoping you'd say something like that. You've always been so... open." He nodded to Lyran. "We have something special planned."

Oh? This sounded like fun.

"Roll over," Falcon said, and I did, flat on my stomach. I lay, relaxing in the sun, as one of them, I couldn't tell which, oiled my rear opening, stimulating it enough that when the toy was inserted it felt thrillingly pleasant.

"Time to get up, hands and knees," Lyran said. I put my butt up first, wiggling it for them before lazily coming to hands and knees. I half expected one of them to be in front of me, but they weren't. Pan was there, looking... curious.

I looked back and Falcon was positioned behind me, half-bent... with Lyran behind him... It took me a moment to realize Lyran was oiling up Falcon's opening as well. Very interesting.

Meanwhile Falcon had a hand down between my legs, fingers moving over my folds getting me worked up again. He didn't have to work hard; I was still riding some of the high from earlier and — though Pan had put my insides back to normal — I was still very loose after Rhino's rough pounding.

As such, Falcon was quickly inside of me, moving with shallow, gentle thrusts. I turned my head back around and was about to close my eyes and enjoy what was to come, when I saw Pan absent-mindedly stroking himself as he watched the two men behind me.

"What are you waiting for?" I asked him. "My mouth is empty, and it shouldn't be."

Pan blinked in shock as I opened my mouth wide, batting my eyelashes at him innocently. He was quickly up on his knees before me. I tilted my head back a little to adjust for him as he filled my mouth with his cock. He didn't even need to thrust, as Falcon was picking up his pace and pushing me forward with each of his movements, which gave me a natural rhythm moving over Pan's cock.

Then I heard Falcon's gasp and he paused for a long moment. I thought I felt little shudders from him, then he was moving again. Only this time with each of his thrusts there came a second harder push just after; two thrusts in one as Lyran plunged into him.

It was... very different from the hard and rough sex with Rhino earlier, but still incredibly stimulating.

My first orgasm was unexpected and sharp. I gasped as the toy in my ass moved and wiggled. Falcon's hand was on my buttocks, and he must have been manipulating it with his thumb, moving it around inside me. I moaned onto Pan's cock as the shockwave of bliss slammed through me, then reverberated like trapped waves, sending tingles down to my fingers and toes.

After that, I just let the ecstasy flow over me and through me. Falcon was big enough that he was already filling me well and hitting my deep-pleasure spot. Several orgasms rose then crashed over me before I heard Falcon's gasping shouts:

"Oh Spirits! Blessed Bloody Spirits!" he cried out, as I guessed he was receiving Lyran's release. And that seemed to cause a chain reaction. He had a moment of hard, deep thrusting before he came as well. I felt as if I was receiving the full force of both men in that one release.

But Pan hadn't come yet. I was weak, but I lifted one arm up between his legs, massaging his sack as I sucked hard on his erection. I flicked my tongue under his head and that was all he needed. He cried out, trembling and moaning, as we all were, with our joined pleasures.

The afternoon continued with various sessions of love and relaxation, and we ate another meal on the hillside as evening fell. After our dinner, we joined again, this last time a bit more desperate and needful. We all knew tomorrow would bring a battle that the odds said we shouldn't win. None of us knew what would happen, and we all wanted to suck the marrow out of these last moments of joy.

The stars were out by the time we returned to town. We'd had our fun, our release, knowing it could possibly be our last. I had no regrets. I was ready for the fight that would come tomorrow.

At least, I hoped I was ready.

CHAPTER 14

ROO

THAT EVENING OUR SCOUTS REPORTED THAT THE DRAGON lord's army was camped just a couple miles away. We kept our own sentries alert and ready in case of subterfuge, but none came.

Ceph slept with me, curled up in my bed, and I held him close. He wept in his sleep, but my presence seemed to soothe his night-terrors. He'd been doing a bit better since our talk, but he was still so very lost and withdrawn.

The next day dawned grey and overcast, as if the world sensed the darkness of what was to come. It rained hard just after dawn, which Lyran said would do wonders for the newly created marsh area at the base of the hill on which the town sat.

Have you ever been to war before? I asked Leoa.

No, nothing like this, a few skirmishes with wild men

from the north in a previous life, but... she trailed off, voice lost to the terrible awe of what we'd face today. *But I'll help you where I can. I know how to fight, and if needed, I can help you defend yourself.*

Thank you, I said. I hoped it wouldn't come to that.

After the rains let up, a heavy mist settled over things. People dispersed to their various battle positions to wait. I knew the basics of the plan, but I was trying not to think about it; about all the things that could go wrong. I was worried for everyone, but I tried to focus on the part I'd play in the coming battle. I wasn't a warrior and would hold no weapon, at least no physical weapon.

I sat, trying to be still and centered, in a room high in one of the buildings facing the battlefield. Ceph was with me. He had armor on and a sword at the ready, but it sat heavily upon him, like some aged and bent warrior. He would protect me, as much as he could. He'd promised that, though I feared all he really sought was the release of death. And I think he hoped that if he died protecting me, that might lend some peace to his soul. I desperately did not want that to happen.

I'll protect him too, if I have to, Leoa added.

I sent her a feeling of gratitude, saying nothing.

"They're coming," he said, looking out the high window of our room.

The mists had parted. A light drizzle fell, but we could see a fair distance from this vantage point.

I sought out into the souls around me. This would be my part: bolstering the spirits of those fighting on our side and bringing down the spirits of our enemy. After that night when fleeing Osera, I knew how to reach into a multitude of souls at once. First, I found our allies. They were in small groups around the town, waiting for their moment to fight. I sent a hint of hope and certainty into each of them, not much but enough to lift their spirits. I needed to conserve my energy. This would be a long day. Then I sought out to the west and felt... I gasped. There were so many of them. Tens of thousands of men in battlelines. I touched each of them, draining their certainty just a bit. I tried not to lose hope, but in that moment it was very easy to find the doubt and despair I wished to send into our foes, since I was feeling it myself.

Then I heard the heavy flap of wings in the distance and my heart nearly gave out. That massive dragon was coming.

This would be Lyran's part of the plan. He needed to distract Aaghar and his dragon for a moment or two, draw the enemy commander away from the battle into a fight of his own. I hoped he'd survive the fight with his brother.

I'm so terribly worried... for all of us! I admitted to Leoa.

Use your own power, bolster your resolve and certainty.

Yes, of course, you're right. I did so, feeling my anxiety fade a little. Still, I couldn't afford to spend much more on myself. I had much to do today.

Lastly, I connected with Dawn. Her role might just be the hardest. She would face Swan. It was much easier to connect with Dawn since yesterday. Whatever she'd done with her spirit had brought us even closer together. Before, I'd always felt our connection, no matter how far apart we were, but now it felt like she was beside me, perhaps even within my own soul, even though she was off on her own.

I sent her hope and courage, peace and certainty. *Be careful, my sister.* Though sister didn't seem to cover the intensity and intimacy of our bond. It was more like we were twins. Two bodies but somehow from one spirit and soul.

And to you, my dearest heart. That shocked me a little. I didn't know we'd actually be able to hear what we sent to each other.

You can hear me?

Yes. A laugh. *This is new.*

Indeed. I... be careful out there, Dawn.

Another laugh. *When have you ever known me to be careful? I shall be myself, that is all I can promise.*

Even though I didn't feel at all mirthful, I laughed a bit as well. *Yes, I suppose you're right. I guess... do what you need to, to live through today.*

And you as well.

I will.

A moment of hesitance then a soft: *Thank you, Roo...for these emotions of support and for... everything. You are truly my heart.*

And you are mine, my beloved friend.

I sensed her growing courage and love, and I knew she was concentrating on the fight to come.

She'll prevail. She always finds a way. Leoa was trying to lift my spirits

I know. We'd worked hard yesterday. I hoped it would be enough to defeat Swan.

"So many," Ceph whispered.

I rose and went to the window with him.

The Thraian army was indeed vast, their lines disappeared into the haze of the distance. They approached to a set point, then stopped. Waiting.

The drizzle turned to rain again.

We'd made sure, the previous night, that none of the enemy scouts had discovered our little swampy surprise. And they'd stopped their advance before finding it... good.

I wondered what they were waiting for... then I heard a dragon's roar and the flap of wings as it passed over the enemy army. A moment later, came a growing thunder of distant horses. From down a central divide in the enemy ranks, came a — seemingly endless — charge of horsemen. They burst forth from the front of the lines and rode hard, fanning out, to charge at our archers on the cusp of the hill.

A flight of arrows was loosed by our men, but it did little, the horsemen were moving too fast. They would have surely run right up the hill and slaughtered our archers... if they hadn't hit the mire we'd made.

Horses whinnied and men screamed as the heavy charge came to a sudden halt. Horses pitched forward, slowed by the muck, and riders were tossed. Then those behind them ran into them or reared. It was chaos. The next volley of arrows from our men on the hill did indeed pelt down along that now-bunched up line of cavalrymen and even more fell. More riders, from the back, tried to fan out further to the sides and see if there was a way around, but they too fell into the swamp and slowed. Some began the laborious slog across the quagmire, but they were easily picked off by our archers. The many horsemen who hadn't reached the swamp, milled about and gathered closer and closer as more came from behind, not knowing the charge had stopped. Again, arrows fell upon them, and horse and rider went down. I didn't want to imagine the fate of a man, thrown by his mount and trampled by others.

I shuddered. These were enemies, but they were still men, and I felt a horrid sadness for the death which would prevail today.

Harden your heart, my child, there will be far more

carnage before the day is through. I know you don't like it, but we must prevail today, which means tens of thousands of men will die.

I said nothing to Leoa's words. I didn't know what to say.

Eventually the horsemen retreated, and the enemy army waited once again.

The rain lifted and the clouds began to part, streamers of sunlight peeking through. But that light did little to lift my mood. The fighting was far from over.

And as I saw that massive dragon land on a nearby hill, I knew another fight was about to start and I sent a bolster of bravery to Lyran, Pan, and Midnight.

"Stay alive," I whispered.

Beside me, Ceph nodded slowly.

CHAPTER 15

LYRAN

THAVRALIAN WAS A DREADFUL TERROR, ESPECIALLY WHEN viewed from the ground. My chest vibrated with the intensity of my pounding heart. All it would take was for Aaghar to decide he didn't want to fight me, and I'd be destroyed in fire. I had to hope he stayed true to his character. He had always loved getting into the fight himself, crushing things with those terrible fists of his, or rending the enemy with his massive sword.

And as we'd hoped, he circled once over us, then Thavralian landed at the far end of the long hill to the north of the battlefield.

I'd seen the massacre of the enemy cavalry, just as planned. We'd stopped their advance... for now. Their generals would be trying to figure out some way to get across that mire we'd created. I smiled, a grim and terrible thing, knowing they'd come to only one conclusion: the only way to fill it in would be with their own dead, cut down by our archers as they tried to cross. Line after line of infantry would be sent to their deaths just so eventually some might make it through. That... or they'd wait for their leader to finish this paltry fight up on the hill, then destroy the village in fire.

I hoped that wouldn't happen.

Aaghar threw himself down from his high saddle, landing easily and drawing his impossibly large sword as he strode toward me.

"You always were cunning, little brother. You've decimated my cavalry, a nice move. I assume you being up here is a challenge? A one-on-one fight to the death, to the victor go the spoils?"

That was exactly what I wanted him to think, but I remained mute, not confirming his words. My honor demanded I not reply; if I agreed to a one-on-one fight, I'd be bound to that, but I hadn't. He just assumed so, but that wasn't the plan. I knew my chances of defeating Aaghar alone were slim. So, I had help.

"One of us will die today," I said, knowing my words would at the same time confirm his thoughts and free me of the burden of honor.

He laughed. "Indeed." Then he roared and charged in at me. He was stronger than I was, but I was quicker... though, not by much. I had to use every ounce of my own strength and speed as well as what

Eophon had gifted to me, to resist Aaghar's vicious attacks. It was all I could do to knock his sword to one side or the other as he swung relentlessly at me, laughing the entire time. I gave ground, backing up, drawing him farther from Thavralian.

I was quickly bathed in sweat, despite the coolness of the damp day. I wasn't tiring yet, but I could feel tension start to build in my muscles.

"You're better than you used to be, little brother. You've been practicing these past few years."

"Indeed." I didn't have much breath for wordy conversations.

"But you must know you can't win. My reach is longer and you daren't get close enough for me to cut you down. You won't even scratch me. And we both know you'll tire long before I do. I'm not even winded yet!"

All of that was true.

I retreated a little farther and saw a set of bushes off to my right from the corner of my eye.

And with one leg back, I stopped giving ground and held. I needed to keep him right here in this spot.

"Ho? What's this now? Growing a backbone? Good, let us fight for real brother!" Aaghar drew back that massive sword high over his head for a heavy cleaving strike down upon me. I had a brief opening upon him but didn't take it. I needed him to do what he was doing and not change his movement. So, I pretended fatigue — it didn't take much — and waited, raising my sword to block the strike he would deliver.

That's when Midnight appeared, leaping high to catch Aaghar's wrist in a crushing blow. She was small but strong, like all Fey.

And speaking of Fey, Pan came scrambling out from those bushes and slashed into the back of Aaghar's left leg, behind the knee. Aaghar screamed and dropped his sword, then fell to one knee. I quickly shifted my block to an attack, hoping to end this quickly. But Aaghar was quick too and a hardened warrior. He dove and rolled to one side, coming up quickly to face the three of us.

"You treacherous bastard!" he roared.

I smiled. "I never said I'd fight you one on one, you just assumed I would. And now your sword is over here, and you're outnumbered. Surrender Aaghar, and I promise your death will be quick." I couldn't keep him alive. He was too much of a symbol, a danger. But I could give him a quick and painless death.

"Never!" he spat. He looked at his right wrist, Midnight had hacked mostly through his bracer and deep into his forearm. It had been enough to weaken his hand to make him drop his sword, but still he bunched that hand into a fist, as he did with his other, and set himself. His left leg was hindering him, he was favoring it, but he was still ready to fight. I warned the others:

"Even disarmed, he's deadly. One hit from those fists could kill any of us."

I set myself as did Midnight and Pan. Midnight vanished again.

Aaghar's eyes darted about, his head cocking, perhaps listening.

"Careful," I warned Midnight. He had advanced senses like mine. "His hearing is keen."

Aaghar smiled. "Let's finish this brother. I'll kill you and these others." His grin widened. "And for your treachery, I'll stop playing fair." He raised his voice to a shout. "Thav! Burn that town to the ground!"

I heard the heavy flap of wings behind me.

Now... it was time for Eophon to play his part. *Go, my friend and tear up that beast!*

I will, Lyran. You do the same.

Aaghar roared and came at me, fists swinging.

He caught the swing from my sword on his heavy bracer, then surged forward. I ducked his fist and slashed again, but his thick armor took the blow.

Pan darted in and slashed at his legs. Aaghar shifted and suddenly I was between Pan and my brother. Another fist headed for me, and it was my turn to block, turning his arm away with my sword.

I heard a sword strike his back, but he didn't react. His armor there would be heavier.

Aaghar spun a kick behind him, and I heard a grunt.

"Midnight?" I called, but there was no answer. I still couldn't see her, and I didn't know if she would become visible again if she was unconscious or dead. Which meant I had to assume she was out of the fight.

Aaghar laughed and pressed his advantage, looming over me, swinging relentlessly. Suddenly I was on the defensive again, Pan always seeming to be stuck behind me.

I deflected Aaghar's massive fists and even managed to land another blow on him, slicing through his armor at a thinner spot near his elbow, but it seemed to slow him little.

He paused and I used the break to strike at him. But his hesitancy had been a feint, and I should have known it. He stopped my sword with his hand. I got through his gauntlet into his palm, but he was able to grasp the blade. Then, he easily yanked the weapon from my grip and snapped it in two. He's sacrificed more of his right hand, which was now bleeding from wrist and palm, but he'd disarmed me.

Flame and Fire!

Pan darted in at him, but Aaghar kicked out and backed the smaller man off. Then with speed I hadn't expected, he jabbed at me. It was an off-the-cuff strike, but still his fist crushed my armor and sent me flying backwards.

I landed hard, skidding a few feet, the breath knocked out of me and my head spinning. Darkness edged over my vision, but I forced myself back, surging my awareness through the pain of my head and body.

I couldn't catch my breath. My breastplate was caved in and pressing hard on my chest. I needed to get it off.

But Aaghar wasn't going to give me that time. He roared his victory and charged at me.

Then Pan was there in front of me, blocking Aaghar's path.

"You'll have to go through me to get to him!" Pan shouted.

Aaghar laughed. "You want to die too, little one? Fine!" The large man lashed out with a kick, a big roundhouse, which should have sent Pan flying, killing him, but Pan leaned into it and stabbed at the same time.

Aaghar and I were both amazed when his kick was stopped by the small man, who grunted, but held his ground. More, Pan had managed to slice into Aaghar's boot, and the large man came away limping more.

"What are you?" Aaghar gasped, shocked.

"I'm the man who's going to kill you," Pan said calmly, then stalked in toward the dragon lord.

CHAPTER 16

FALCON

"I sense Swan," Dawn said nearby. "She's coming." She turned to me. "Good-bye my love, stay alive and I promise I will as well."

I kissed her, quick and intense, before she began to make her way to the south end of the town and down the hill. She knew Swan was coming for her, so she'd draw the crazed woman away from the fighting as much as possible.

I turned back to the men I was commanding, two hundred archers, waiting for the enemy to advance so they could rain down arrows upon them.

I saw that colossal, fear-inspiring dragon lift off from the hill to the north and east and I hoped Pan and Lyran were doing well.

And in the next instant, I hoped I'd be well, as that massive dragon made straight for us. Its first strafe of

fire would burn us all to cinders in one go... unless
things went to plan. But I couldn't see Eophon, who
was supposed to be protecting us, so my heart raced
faster and faster as I shouted for my archers to hold
their ground in the face of that massive beast. I saw the
dragon's chest swell with an inhalation as fire began to
lick at the edges of its mouth. Then he banked and
dove at us, and it was all I could do not to run. I
couldn't fault the few men who did indeed run.

Fire belched out of the great dragon's mouth and
poured down... to hit another form, flying along below
it. Eophon's invisible form soaked up the entire burst
of fire, then it became visible, and our archers cheered
a great and heartfelt 'hoorah' of relief; I couldn't help
but join them.

The two dragons began to battle with tooth and
claw, circling higher into the sky, which spared us more
attacks from the enemy's dragon.

*Of all the things I wish to experience, being burned
alive by dragon-fire, isn't one of them,* Eluei said with a
sigh of relief.

Agreed, I replied. *Eophon saved us.*

I could kiss that dragon.

Is that an experience you truly wish for?

*First, let's survive today, then we'll talk about kissing
dragons.*

Done.

And... not long after, just as Lyran had predicted,

horns sounded from the enemy army. Their generals knew they'd get no help from their prince, nor his dragon. They'd have to take this village the hard way.

The infantry marched forward, over the corpses of the dead cavalry men... and into our treacherous swamp.

Interestingly, the first row of men into the mire, sunk deep, up to their necks, crouching low as they slogged slowly through the deep mud. A solid strategy that would give us less of a target to hit. They also held their shields above their heads to protect them from arrows.

I changed my next command. "Aim high, for those not yet in the swamp!" I called and the command was echoed down the line. At this point we'd be better served hitting those bunching up on the banks of the wetlands. Archers raised their bows a little, then I commanded them to fire. We could allow a few of the enemy to cross the muck to get to us. That was what the Njorvasoturi and Karhukora were waiting for. They were still hidden, ready to charge in.

"Make your shots count!" I shouted. I knew there was little most of our archers could do at this distance. If they had been trained for years, they might have a chance of hitting what they were aiming for, but most of those here had only been practicing for a few weeks. We would simply drop as many arrows on the foes as we could and... hope.

"Draw... and... fire!" I commanded. The first line of infantry wasn't even halfway through the swamp yet, several other lines dropping in behind them, but we were felling dozens of men with each of our volleys and every man who didn't cross the mire was one we didn't have to fight, once we were out of arrows.

But that was still some time off. We'd sent fewer than twenty volleys so far, less than one tenth of our arrows.

"Draw... and... fire!" I called as the enemy army bunched closer and closer on the far side of the swamp.

Yet, even with the hundreds we'd killed so far... the enemy still extended out as far as I could see.

I felt through my bond with Swift. He was still very distant to the east.

Come on, brother. We need you to come through with this! I sent him a feeling of urgency and need through our link. His quest had been to return to Elista and find a man in Dawn's mother's family. A man who could jump great distances in the blink of an eye... then to bring as many men as possible back with him.

But... if he hadn't found Lord Fin yet...?

I prayed to the Spirits he had, and that they were nearly ready to jump here. If they didn't... I feared we'd lose the day, even with all our planning and effort.

Please brother...

"Draw... and... fire!"

The lines of infantry in the muck were just past halfway, moving slowly, but steadily. I judged there were eighty to a hundred men in each long line. If two of those lines formed up and stormed our hill, we'd have an even number of their infantry and our archers. We'd not last long.

But I couldn't lose hope now. We had a job to do, and it was to kill as many of their men as possible.

"Draw... and... fire!"

To my left I saw a swan descending from the sky.

Do you think I could hit her from here? I asked Eluei. In one of her previous lives her True-Bonded had been quite good with a bow.

We can try, that would be quite the shot though.

Caught up with a need to help Dawn, I took my bow and aimed for the beast. She was some distance off, and still high, but... when I next commanded my men to fire, I loosed my arrow at her. It caught a wing, sending some feather's flying but didn't seem to hurt the swan over-much.

I found it interesting that Swan's protections didn't seem to have helped her in this form... or perhaps she hadn't been expecting an attack? Either way, I was just happy I'd hit her, even if it had done little. Let her know others were watching.

I turned my attention back to the enemy.

The infantry were a dozen feet from the end of the swamp.

"Draw... and... fire!"

Still our arrows peppered down on those heading into the mire, and more and more men fell. But would it be enough?

Volley after volley we sent, and then... the infantry were finally out of the muck and forming up on our side; first one line, then two. They didn't attack yet, waiting. A third line joined them, then a fourth and fifth.

My heart pounded, waiting for the impending call to attack. Still, they waited until a full ten lines had climbed out of the muck, close to a thousand men.

That's when a horn sounded.

"Keep firing over them!" I commanded. We didn't want to hit our own men when... "Sound the charge!" One of our horns sounded.

And like there had been earlier that day, a heavy pounding, thunderous roar began. This one seemed to be all around us. Then, twenty of those massive Karhukora came charging out from the town, ten from either side of our archers, and swarmed down the hill and across in front of us. Each held three Njorvasoturi, one rider and two warriors strapped to the side to cut down any men around them. Behind them came roughly fifty of Lyran's men per side, on horseback, shouting with war-cries as they finally joined the battle.

Despite their vastly fewer numbers, the northerners were fierce and had surprised the Thraian men. They crushed the thousand-man infantry like so much wheat before them. Their pincer charge catching the warriors from the side and driving through them.

The Thraians scattered. Most were cut down, but a few reached the top of the hill. We had a few reserves of swordsmen — fewer than fifty men — who were ready to meet them and defend our archers. They took care of the stragglers easily enough.

And just like that, a thousand of the enemy lay dead or dying upon the hill below us.

But my elation at that victory was quickly tempered. Even if our arrows had killed another thousand more... that was still only two percent of their army.

I swallowed.

The day — and the fighting — was far from over.

CHAPTER 17

RHINO

I TRIED TO STILL MY BREATHING AND CALM MYSELF. I wanted to appear assured and brave to my men. But the truth was: with each line of the enemy that marched by, I felt more and more despair creep into my soul.

I, along with a troop of a hundred of our best warriors — mostly those who had been with Lyran initially and also a few others who'd been the most promising new recruits — waited hidden in the forest to the south of the battlefield. We were on the other side of the swamp from the rest of our forces, alone, with no support, no reinforcements, no help. Our mission was simple: harry the enemies in a surprise attack from their flank.

We were to start with arrows from our hidden position in the forest, then move out to attack their side.

The hope was to do considerable damage before retreating into the forest and getting them to follow us. We'd laid all manner of traps and pitfalls amongst the trees. If we could take out a thousand men, we'd have done our job. It wasn't much, but we wanted the foes to think our forces were more numerous than they were, and all around them, so as to spread fear.

And with the cavalry charge of the Njorvasoturi upon the hill, we'd been given our signal to attack. The enemy was focused ahead.

I gave the hand signal which prompted my men, all down the line to raise their bows, each knowing to do so, because the man beside them was raising his. We wanted this to be a surprise, so there would be no shouted commands.

I dropped my hand and a V-shaped wedge of arrows exploded out from the woods. They had standing orders at this point. Launch three volleys as quick as they could, then drop bows and ready sword and shield.

The three volleys landed well among the marching infantry before us, and many men fell. There were shouts of surprise and pain.

Then I roared a war cry, and the others followed my lead, charging out of the forest into the ranks of the enemy.

I'd spent many hours honing my technique of hitting, then transforming to my avatar. I did so now, becoming a scourge upon my foes, a pestilence which felled them three or more at a time with my great sword. I was the pinnacle of our advance and the men beside me were cutting down more Thraians, who were still reeling from this surprise attack.

But that wouldn't last long.

Horns sounded.

A whole massive chunk of the infantry turned from their froward march to face us.

"Retreat!" I called. But I stayed a little longer to make sure my men made it away. I fought on, hacking through the enemy like wheat before a scythe. And only when they began to advance, did I transform and follow my men back into the forest.

Their orders were to pick up their bows again, and retreat into the depths, avoiding our own traps. We didn't have many arrows, only ten per man. So, they were to use them only when they had a good shot, to take down the enemy or to steer them into our pitfalls.

I wasn't much good with a bow myself, so I stayed at the fringes of the wood, keeping up my transforming and attacking in sequence.

The enemy entered the forest, marching slowly and carefully, but their lines couldn't keep shape, as they had to move around the trees.

The first few arrows were loosed and the enemy, as hoped, began to group up a bit more, heading into what seemed like open 'alleys' between trees that we had cleared out. It looked like an easy path.

Then came the first screams as men fell into shallow pits of sharpened stakes or were caught up in — what had once been — fisherman's nets and dragged up into the trees.

I found a clump of soldiers and landed next to them, attacking with a roar. They had no clue what I was, nor where I'd come from. They all died quickly. I vanished back into my beetle form and flew to another group.

On and on I went, moving through the forest. I took injuries, a few serious enough to make me consider stopping the fight, but... I kept moving, bloody and growing tired, I cut down as many men as I could. I heard cries of "demon!" and "magic!" but still no one was expecting me when I showed up.

And when I finally joined the remaining men of my troop on the far side of the forest, next to the river, the enemy was shredded and fleeing. I didn't know how many we'd killed, but it had to have been several hundred. And as I looked at my men, we'd only lost perhaps twenty of our number.

One of them ran to me and began bandaging my wounds.

"Do we flee across the river?" a man asked, and I sensed the true question in his voice. Our orders were to do only what we had just done, harry the enemy then flee back. But we'd done so well... these men wanted to continue the fight.

As do I, Iomu growled savagely within me. *We're far from dead and I can lend you strength, not that you need it. Let's destroy as many of these bastards as we can!*

I considered for along moment. *You think we can really do it?*

I think we can take a whole lot of them with us before we go.

But it's a suicide mission.

And?

I laughed at Iomu's frivolous disregard for my life. *You'll live on after this, I won't.*

You'll live on in me and my memories, Iomu said and almost sounded sympathetic. *Now let's kill those bastards!*

I don't know why, but I'm with you.

"I'll not make any of you fight. We've done what we came to do," I said calling out to my men. "But I am not done killing those bastards, and if any of you wish to join me, I say we go keep nibbling at their flanks." I gave a grim smile. "If we do... we go knowing we probably won't return." I swallowed hard at that. "But we also go, knowing every man we kill here is one less that might gain that hill and take the village where our families and loved ones are also fighting."

There were grunts and murmurs, nods and head-shakes. "Who's with me?" I asked.

Well over half of the men remaining raised their hands.

"The rest of you, get across the river and get back to the village if you can. Protect our families. The rest of us... we'll cause some infernal chaos among the enemy."

Pits yes, we will! Iomu shivered with expectant glee... bloodthirsty little Lumani that she was.

A cheer went up, and the two groups separated. I led my men back into the fray. Suddenly my wounds hardly hurt at all. I felt invincible, like I could do anything, and I could see in the eyes of those with me, they felt it too.

We marched to our doom with grim smiles upon our faces.

Let the enemy come. Let them fall upon our swords.

Today we might die, but our story would be told for ages to come!

CHAPTER 18

DAWN

With the strengthening of my spirit-gift that I'd done yesterday, I could feel Swan as she drew nearer.

I'd moved to the banks of the river, south of Dwa Brody. I had my weapons with me, but if this went well, I wouldn't need them. All I would need is my spirit and the guts to stand before Swan and hope she wouldn't incinerate me instantly. She wanted to kill me in front of my mother, which meant capturing me alive. I hoped that was still her goal and she hadn't changed her mind. If I'd become too much trouble...

Don't think about that, concentrate on what is to come, Amya advised. *I'll help you as much as I can.*

Thanks, I'll need it.

I heard the flap of her wings and looked up to see the swan descending. I reached into her spirit and tried to connect with her gift. All my practice the day before helped. I could feel it inside of her, but I sensed instantly I'd not just be able to grab it and pull it from her. Even within her own spirit, that foul gift protected itself. I would have to push through several unseen barriers to get to it. But I was far stronger in the realm of spirit than in the physical realm. I could never hope to penetrate her external shields, but her spirit-shields I could overpower, it would just take time.

"Hello, Little Bitch." It sounded like she'd made that her name for me. It wasn't wholly inappropriate. "You're waiting for me. You knew I'd come for you. Didn't want to get your friends involved this time? Smart. Does that mean you'll come quietly?"

"If I do, will you stop this war?" I didn't intend to go with her, but I might as well keep her talking.

"Ah... yeah, sure."

"You don't have any control over those troops, do you?"

She grinned and shrugged. "No."

"Then what's my incentive to come with you? Your hospitality last time was a bit lacking."

"What's a little torture between enemies? Now, are you coming? I suppose I could go up into that village and wreak some havoc or kill your friends. Would you like that instead? I haven't wreaked havoc in a while."

I was through the first layer of shields around her spirit-gift, almost there!

I tried supplication. "No, please, don't do that!" I hoped I sounded desperate enough.

She cocked her head, eyes squinting. "You're stalling, waiting for something? What is it? Whatever it is, it's not going to work. Nothing can hurt me!"

We'd see about that.

I drew my sword. "What if I'd found a way to cut through that shield of yours?" I asked, putting on a wily grin.

Her brow furrowed, eyes narrowing further. "Impossible."

I played out the bluff. "Want to find out?"

She backed up a step.

Careful not to spook her, we need her here, Amya whispered within me.

I know, but I also need to keep her from incapacitating me, which means keeping her unsteady. We'll see if this gambit works.

I laughed. "I thought you said it was impossible, that you're invincible?" I threw her words back at her. "What's the harm in letting me take one swing."

She looked around, clearly suspicious now, but there was no one there. "You're up to something. I can feel it."

"Just one little stab. What could it hurt?"

She backed up another step.

I was so close to breaking down her barriers and getting into her spirit-gift, just a few more seconds. "Afraid of me now?" I asked stepping forward.

She backed up again, but I could see in her eyes, I'd spooked her. She was clearly afraid of some sneak attack or hidden ally, even though the only place they could possibly hide would be in the water of the river not far away, or high up on the hill in the town to my right.

"You're not worth it," Swan said backing up again. "I'll go help my lover's army crush the rest of you, then maybe you'll come willingly when you have nothing left in your life. Yes, I like that idea. I hope you've said your goodbyes, Dawn. Soon all your friends will be dead!" She turned and veered into a swan.

But that was apparently what I needed. Some of her protections shifted, altered, lowered, in the split second as she changed shapes, and I broke through to grasp her spirit gift. She lifted off, starting to fly away, but I grabbed and pulled.

The swan squawked loudly and shuddered in the air, crumpling a little, falling and flapping, landing awkwardly.

Swan transformed back, rolling on the ground to face me. "What is this? What did you do?"

I laughed, finally having the upper hand on her. "I'm taking your spirit gift," I said with a grin.

Her eyes went wide, I saw the unbridled panic on

her face. "No!" And she blasted her red energy at me. I couldn't stop it; I hadn't fully extinguished her gift yet. I knew it would incinerate me.

My heart lurched, and I leaped.

CHAPTER 19

FALCON

That was it, the last flight of arrows.

The archers in the long line nearby were putting down their bows and picking up various different weapons, whatever melee-instrument they were best with. The Njorvasoturi were in the midst of doing another crushing cavalry ride upon their Karhukora, but they were depleted, four of the massive bear-like animals were dead upon the field. The Thraian infantry just kept coming, like a massive wave, and still, I couldn't see the end of them. But... I did notice there had been a time where the lines coming at us had only been half as long... Rhino's work, I guessed. Hopefully he'd survived his raid.

I drew my sword and sent the command for retreat. We'd back up to the town now. We knew it better than the attackers and we'd set up barricades and dead-end-alleys where we could ambush them. Now the fight began in truth, and I hoped we'd be able to hold.

How many do you think we've taken out? I asked Eluei.

At least ten thousand men, perhaps as many as twenty thousand? It's hard to tell, but between our archers and the Njorvasoturi, we've done well.

Twenty thousand? That's a fifth of their forces! And we'd only lost perhaps forty men. I felt a moment of elation at this. *Even that much is a massive victory!* Things had gone as well as we could have hoped, so far…

Eluei was a bit more sober when she said: *They still have at least eighty thousand men to send against us.*

I sighed. *Yeah, I know.* Looking up to gauge the sun, I found not much time had passed. It hadn't taken us long to go through forty-thousand arrows. Yet, already, I felt like I'd been fighting for days! And there was much more to come.

The Njorvasoturi sounded their retreat. They too would return to the village and the other surprises we had planned there.

The two hundred men who had been archers now broke into small groups of five to ten men. I led one of these and we bolted down an alley to a choke point we'd made of scrap metal and refuse. It would force the enemy to come through one at a time. We filed through carefully avoiding the jagged metal edges of the rough-cut roofing we'd used to block the alley.

Then we waited.

We heard the enemy approaching slowly. They weren't charging in.

The long haft of a spear came through our choke-point first, trying to jab to either side. I slashed and removed the tip when it came near me. The wielder of the spear drew it back and another tried to poke as best it could around the corner.

Something was up. They were being careful, which made sense, but...

I looked up to see men half-over the jagged topped barrier. They'd thought to try coming over the top.

"Above!" I shouted.

Our own spearmen reacted instantly jabbing at those coming over the walls, one took a spear-tip through his face and died, flopping on the barrier. That would actually make it easier for the next man to come over, so I jumped up on some boxes we'd stacked behind the blockage and pushed the dead man back and off.

Apparently having their ruse interrupted, the enemy decided to give us what we wanted. One man dove through the opening, followed quickly by others.

The man who dove through came up to find other spearmen ready and was quickly down. The men behind him faced our swords.

And suddenly we were in the midst of it, a nasty fight. Four of us holding that opening while two spearmen watched the tops of the walls on either side and another two waited in reserve to spell out one of us in the breach or to catch any enemies who happened to make it through us.

We ground through them for what seemed like hours before two of my men were down. That was our signal to retreat. I gave the call.

We bolted to the next obstacle as the enemy began pouring — still one at a time — out of the gap behind us. As we ran, we pulled out the wooden cover over the pit we'd put right on the other side of the choke point. Three or four men had made it through, but the rest after that would have to try to jump the hole or carefully navigate down and through it. Or they could take the time to dismantle our barrier; either way, we'd have a moment.

We turned a corner, waited and when the few men behind us, came around they died quickly. Then we removed the cover of another pit just at that corner and retreated up ladders to the rooves of the surrounding houses. There was a tall barrier at the end of the alley around the corner and we'd stashed a few extra arrows up here, just for this type of fighting. It wasn't much, five arrows per man, but it would harrow the enemy even more before we moved to our next trap.

One of my men crept to the side of the roof, above where our previous barrier was and kept watch, silently signaling us when men were coming. Some fell into the second pit, some jumped it, or made their way around it on the thin ledge of earth. And those we picked off with carefully aimed shots.

"They're on the rooves!" someone shouted from below.

And that was it, we needed to flee now. If they had ladders or other ways to get up here, we were finished. So, we fled down trap doors in those buildings, descending through before putting them to the torch. Let them come to the rooves and die in the conflagration we were setting.

Down the line of buildings facing that side of the hill, I could see other fires starting. We had a moment then to catch our breaths and young men and women came running with water and bandages. I'd made it out with seven of my men still alive and doing well, two dead, and one injured enough that he'd not be fighting much. He was helped away by a few other non-combatants. Depending on how the day went, he might be fighting again, but if he was, it would mean the rest of us were dead. I didn't want to think of that option.

Another runner came to me with a tally: "Twenty-three men lost or injured. The Njorvasoturi are in place for their part."

I nodded to the young woman. "Thank you."

Twenty-three, that was more than ten percent. I didn't know how many of the enemy we'd killed, but if we kept losing men at this rate, we'd be down to the bare bones soon enough.

We retreated to the next line of buildings across a wide avenue. That would be our next kill-zone. We'd hide with our remaining arrows to snipe men who survived the rushes of the Njorvasoturi down that long road. We still had a few tricks up our sleeves, but soon enough we'd be down to simply fighting man to man, and once that happened, we'd be done.

I felt for Swift. He was still far to the east.

"Come quickly, brother," I whispered. "Or you won't have a brother to save."

With a moment or two still before the buildings were burned and the enemy would advance, I went to see Roo, high up in one of the buildings, overlooking the battle. I entered the room to find Ceph at the window looking out. He quickly looked back at me, then slumped in relief.

"She concentrates still," he said softly.

Roo was on the floor between us, sitting cross-legged, eyes closed. Sweat dampened her long hair, and she was trembling slightly.

"Anything from your brother?" Ceph asked.

I shook my head. Swift was the lynchpin in our plan. Right now, Roo would be keeping a low level of emotional drain on the enemy. She could sap the spiritual strength from all of them, but that would do us little good if we didn't have an army of our own to mop them up. Our small force here wouldn't have been able to deal with a hundred thousand men before they began to come around and fight again. Which meant, we needed another force, the force Swift had gone to get.

"I hope he gets here soon," Ceph said.

I had to agree. "Take care of her," I said to Ceph.

He nodded, even though he looked like he could barely take care of himself. "And you take care of all of us," he whispered.

"I will."

I left, returning to my men.

A runner came to report: "The enemy has started to surround the village. They mean to attack from all sides."

I nodded. We'd expected that after this frontal assault was halted by fire. We'd blocked off all but a few ways into the village. They'd come and we'd face them.

This is it, Eluei said. *The final act. I... I love you, Falcon. It's been a joy to be your True-Bonded and—*

And you will be for years to come, I said, though I was putting up a brave front and she knew it.

Because if Swift didn't arrive soon... nothing would save us.

CHAPTER 20

ROO

I TREMBLED WITH THE EFFORT OF MAINTAINING CONTACT with the enemy multitudes, and the dwindling number of our own troops. I tried, where possible, to take any sense of victory and hope from the enemy and instill it in the defenders, but that was growing harder and harder.

Keep it up, you're doing so well, Leoa cheered me on, but I sensed her fatigue in addition to my own. It was just all so... overwhelming.

"They're everywhere," Ceph breathed. They're in the village and... I can't see the Njorvasoturi anymore." He was trying to keep me appraised of the situation, but I knew. The enemy had flooded into the village and was quickly overwhelming our few remaining troops. And connected as I was to all of them, I felt the deaths, the sudden and painful end to that bundle of emotions: mostly fear and a desperate need to live.

Tears traced my cheeks, adding to the sweat which already streaked over my face.

Heavy booted footfalls out in the corridor interrupted my work.

"Pits!" Ceph swore and I felt him go from the window to the door.

I felt those outside. They were not allies. "Enemies!" I warned Ceph and broke off from my concentration to look at him. He was terrified, shaking. I sent him courage and resolve. He stopped trembling, facing the door as it opened.

I'd seen Ceph fight before, swift and deadly. As these foes rushed in, he was a shadow of his former self, sluggish and weak, but still... he moved faster than they did, slicing and cutting them up.

But more kept coming. A full score of men surging into the room.

"She's mine!" one of them yelled, spying me. "Spoils of w—" Ceph slit the man's throat even as he tried to make for me.

But Ceph couldn't take them all. Perhaps if he'd been his former self, he might have, but as he was now, he managed to cut down fourteen men and seriously wound four others before a sword took him in the belly and he fell back. Thankfully — for him at least — the men didn't seem as interested in finishing him off as they did... in me. Only two men remained, stalking toward me with hunger in their eyes; faces covered in blood.

Ceph pushed his sword across the floor to me. I grabbed it, standing and backing away from the two men. But these men must have been able to see I didn't know how to fight. I had some training, but a sword was not my preferred weapon and I held it awkwardly in both hands.

"Put down the blade, girlie, and Hobs and I promise we won't be too rough with you. It's been a long trip here and a long fight and we just want some company. Give us a good time and we'll treat you well enough, protect you from others."

"Yeah." The other nodded. "But if you fight us, if you cut us, we won't be so nice. We'll make sure it hurts and when we're done, we'll hand you around to every other man in the army. So, just relax and let it happen."

Black Pits! No way would I let them touch me.

I can fight them, are you ready? Leoa prompted.

Yes. I pushed fatigue and fear into both of them and they halted, stunned.

Leoa attacked, using my body. We managed to hit the one of them at the base of his neck and the sword bit deep enough to kill him almost instantly, blood spraying everywhere as he fell back.

The other staggered away from me. "What's... happening...?" he whispered.

With Leoa still controlling me, we charged at him, but he'd seen me kill his friend, and his emotions had spiked back to wariness and fear. He managed a block, then swung at me. I felt the tip of his blade slice across my stomach, not deep, but the shock of pain caused me to stagger back as blood stained my dress.

"I'll kill you, bitch," the man hissed and surged forward. Leoa kept him at bay, but even with her skill, I was physically drained from my work and my arms weren't used to this sort of struggle. He would beat past our defenses soon enough.

He knocked my sword down and away, out of one hand. Leoa wouldn't be able to get it up in time to block his next attack.

I'm sorry Roo! Leoa gasped.

The man slashed at me.

At the same time, I saw Ceph throw a helmet, which caught the man on his leg, turning him slightly so his blade only just brushed my right shoulder. I plucked up my sword and, with all my strength, I swung at his chest. I hit armor mostly, but I managed to knock the man down and with my next breath I reversed my sword and fell upon him driving the blade down into his face.

He cried out — very briefly — as I hit him. Yet, his body kept flailing and flinching for many long moments after he died.

Horrified at what I'd done, I scurried back and away, eyes wide with shock.

"You... had... to," Ceph said, wheezing, not doing well at all. He looked pale and far too much blood pooled around him. He needed to be healed soon, but Pan was far away in another fight.

I went to him and did what I could, easing his emotions and seeking bandages to bind him.

"I'll be well," he whispered, once I was close. "Even without my gift, I can heal. Octopuses are good at that."

"Unless more men come," I said, worried.

"Then you'll deal with them, like you did with those two."

I didn't want to think about that. I was on the verge of being sick if I did.

Then... I felt something.

Rising suddenly, I went to the window.

The day had cleared a little, sun over most of the fields now and... there... in the distance there were men wearing a different color: blue and grey, the colors of Elista.

"Swift," I breathed.

But if so, I had something I needed to do.

Ignoring my own pain — clamping my hands on the rough wood of the windowsill to help — I reached out once again to all the enemies around me. So many, thousands upon thousands, but I spread my awareness out like a net. And, once I had them all, I used every ounce of energy I had left to pull at their emotions, leaving them empty and stunned, tired and confused. I pulled and pulled and pulled until I'd drained them all, but that drained me as well and I collapsed against the wall below the window.

"Please..." I whispered. "Be enough."

CHAPTER 21

SWIFT

I felt the world spin around me, disorienting and confusing, before seeing the light of day once again, far from where I had been. This was the spirit-gift of Fin, one of the queen's generals.

I'd found him quick enough, but it had taken time to assemble the army we needed to bring. We'd also needed to find a True-Bonded with telepathy, to share the location in my mind with Fin.

With us, we'd brought the largest army of Elistans we could gather on such short notice. Nearly two thousand men and women, ready for a fight. Most of the men we'd brought were normal army-men, not Nobles. Perhaps twenty True-Bonded Nobles had come with us.

We arrived, holding hands in one long snaking line. Fin quickly released my hand and was away again. There were more men ready to help fight. We'd arrived at the place I'd scouted, behind the enemy lines. The sounds of fighting could be heard in the distance, and the town of Dwa Brody was in flames.

Spirits! I hoped I wasn't too late. If Roo had been killed and couldn't pacify the enemy then I'd just doomed these allies to death.

I veered and took to the skies, as the tentative army advanced slowly behind the enemy. I could see the churned-up farmlands over which the enemy had trod and... a small group fighting a desperate battle well behind the enemy lines.

I swooped down to take a quick survey of the fight. A group of perhaps a dozen men — led by Rhino — were fighting a desperate battle against a group of nearly a hundred times their number.

I flew as fast as I could back to the Elistan lines and transformed. "Follow me quickly!" I shouted and veered into a swift once more. The army surged up behind the enemy and swarmed over them, quickly overpowering them

I reached Rhino as he slumped to the ground, weeping — what I hoped were — tears of joy.

"Thank the Spirits!" he said, between heavy breaths. "We couldn't have lasted much longer. How many did you bring?"

"Almost two thousand from Elista, and another

fifteen hundred heavy cavalry from Vauphan are on their way."

In fact, I could hear their thundering approach. Fin had gotten them here quickly. They had been warned of the swamp lands, but they charged past our position and began to fall upon the rear of the enemy.

And that's when I felt it, Roo's pacification of the enemy. I saw its effects as well, a few of the enemies who'd survived our attack slumped down, near to lifeless.

"Roo is alive," I breathed, and suddenly I needed to be where she was.

"Take me with you," Rhino said, clearly sensing my need to be away.

I looked at him. He was covered in blood, soaked in it, and not all of it was from the enemy. He sported several deep wounds, but still somehow stood.

"Are there healers?" I called to the Elistans around me.

A woman stepped forward. "I can accelerate a person's natural..." She trailed off looking at Rhino. She shook her head. "If you're planning on going anywhere, I can't heal you. You'd be knocked out for a week." She softly added: "How are you still alive?"

Rhino grinned. "Tougher than I look." Then to me. "Let's go." He veered and I did as well. He couldn't fly as fast as I, so I caught his avatar up in one of my feet and swooped quickly toward the village.

Before we got there, I spotted Dawn and Swan to the south, near the river, clutching at each other, locked in some deadly, fierce, struggle.

Should I help her?

I hadn't really been asking Isoa, but they answered anyway. *The fact that she is fighting Swan so far from everyone else is probably because it was meant to be that way. I don't know why, but perhaps Dawn thought of some way to fight the madwoman? Certainly, Dawn is still alive and seems to be handling herself well. But I don't know, what do you think? Should we help her?*

Now wasn't one of the times for Isoa to ramble her observations. Yet, she was probably right, if Dawn was there alone, she probably meant to be. As much as I might want to help her, my presence may actually hinder her, but... I just didn't know. *We'll get to the village and drop Rhino off, maybe he knows what's going on. Then, if we can, we'll help Dawn.*

Sounds like a plan to me.

I darted for the village, where it looked like a massacre had taken place. Bodies piled on top of each other were everywhere, a few people staggering around listlessly.

I dove to one of the few clear spots, dropped Rhino and transformed. Quickly I asked Rhino: "Is Dawn meant to be alone?"

He nodded. "Yes, she found a way to hopefully steal a person's spirit-gift and is trying to take Swan's."

That sounded horrible and hopeful all at the same time. But as long as she knew what she was doing then we'd look for the others first. "Where's Roo?"

Rhino began to stagger off. "She should be this way." He led the way, moving hastily despite his wounds.

We got to the room high in one of the buildings to find a scene of more blood and death. A score of men lay dead or dying and among them, Ceph sat propped against a wall, a big bloody wound in his gut. Roo was limp and lifeless on the far side of the room also slumped against the wall and half lying on the floor. She also had a belly-wound, but it didn't look as fatal as Ceph's. I rushed to Roo as Rhino went to Ceph.

"He's alive, somehow."

I checked Roo. She was breathing, thank the spirits. But if she was unconscious then her draining effect wouldn't last long. "She's alive too."

The earth shuddered and jumped beneath me. Shocked, I rose to look out the window.

The unmoving form of a massive dragon lay amidst the charred ruins of the other half of the town. Above me another dragon roared their triumph. Eophon had won his dragon's duel.

"Swift?" I turned. Falcon was in the doorway. "I felt your arrival. Thank the Spirits. Did you bring an army?"

"Two small ones, but it should be sufficient if the enemy remains down long enough."

Falcon nodded. He didn't look well, covered in blood and injuries, like Rhino. He collapsed in the doorway and closed his eyes. "I... I should help my men clean up." He gave a harsh laugh. "I mean... my man." Then he whispered: "So many dead."

"Stay here, brother, look after Roo and Ceph... and Rhino. I'll do the clean-up," I said. And made to leave.

Falcon's hand caught mine as I passed him. He looked up to me with eyes full of fatigue and pain, but also a gratitude so deep I felt I could see his soul. "Thank you," he said quietly. "You saved us."

I squeezed his hand, then left quickly, hoping to take care of as many of the enemy as I could before they roused.

CHAPTER 22

PAN

AAGHAR ROARED WITH A FERAL FURY AS HIS DRAGON FELL upon the village... dead.

As terrified as I was, I was thankful for the brief respite from his onslaught upon me. I'd been fighting him alone for what seemed like hours, though I knew it hadn't even been a full hour yet. Still, I was at my limits, exhausted and my body pounded with a constant ache from the — I'd lost count how many — hits upon me. It seemed my hide, near-to-impenetrable as it was, could take a few hits from those punishing fists of Aaghar's. Still, I'd be one full-body bruise after all of this, but that was assuming I lived through what was to come.

My sword was broken, and I wielded only the jagged-bladed stub still attached to the hilt. I was breathing ragged breaths and struggling just to stand.

I didn't know if this new rage of Aaghar's would hinder him or make him even stronger. I feared I'd not be able to handle him if he grew stronger still. I needed help.

But Midnight hadn't been seen since early on in the fight, and Lyran still seemed to be struggling after that one punch against him. He'd removed his caved-in breastplate but had yet to stand. I guessed he had more than a few broken ribs. So, I'd been keeping Aaghar busy on my own. The trouble was, I was too small. I couldn't get close to the large man. My reach with a broken blade was far less than that of his long arms, and far less than his legs if he kicked out at me. And it was his kicks I most feared. He'd hit me once with a solid kick to the side and my ribs still ached. I was certain a few ribs were fractured if not broken. Even with all my toughness, his kicks were still far too powerful. Another solid kick, and I might not survive.

But then, Aaghar was looking pretty rough himself. We'd hit him with several good blows before the tides had turned. His right fist was bathed in blood. Any hits upon me from that arm had been weaker. Most of the hits we'd gotten in on him were to his right arm: wrist, elbow, and palm. Other than that, he still limped from my initial strike to his leg. And, I'd had one good strike during our one-on-one fight. I'd managed a stab, low in his gut, just under his breastplate. I wasn't sure how deep, but I could see the blood welling there. That had been the last attack with my full sword. He'd smashed the blade and pulled it out while laughing. This man was a beast... but then... so was I.

This fight was at its end, one way or another. Either I'd die or... some miracle would happen.

I'm here, I'll give you everything I have, Eona said, stalwart, though I feared she'd already given me all she could. *We Lumani were made to be miracles. Trust in that. We'll survive this... somehow.*

That *somehow* wasn't so reassuring.

Yet, I'd already had one minor miracle in the form of this short break. Aaghar was still raging... which meant.... he was open. I should have realized that sooner, but I'd been too fatigued to think straight.

I let out a war cry and dove in between his legs. Rolling, I came up just behind him. I stabbed my jagged blade into the calf of his already injured leg, I needed to weaken it further. I was just a little surprised that he hadn't moved, hadn't evaded this strike. Apparently, he really was incapacitated for a moment. I felt my blade sink deep.

I grinned.

Miracle one, Eona cheered within me.

Then a bloody hand grasped my hair and yanked me off my feet, pulling me up so fast I let go of my sword. It was still stuck in his leg, which was good, but I didn't have it, which was bad.

Aaghar had grabbed me with his 'weak' arm, his

hot blood dripping over my face as he lifted me before him. There was madness in his eyes, a raving and wild look. "You killed my dragon!" he roared at me, spittle flying from his lips. Then he gave a demented smile. "But you've lost now. All these wounds upon me will heal in time... but you—" He gave a manic laugh. "— You won't be able to heal from this, little one!" He drew his other fist back.

This was it, my end.

He hammered his fist into my face. I felt my nose shatter as my world exploded in pain and streamers of light. Yet, I was stunned and surprised that I was alive and still conscious as he pulled the hand back. I spat out a few teeth, blinking, dazed, knowing I'd not be able to see much longer, both of my eyes would be swollen shut soon.

"By The Sacred Flame!" he hissed. "You...?" He too was amazed I'd survived. "Well, you won't survive this!" He brought his other hand to my head, grabbing me with both hands as he swung me down, bringing his knee up to smash my head.

I closed my eyes and prayed to the Spirits.

But the hit never came. Instead Aaghar screamed, and I was tossed to one side.

I landed hard, rolling a few times.

I'd not last much longer; darkness closing in on me, but I forced myself up. It was adrenaline which kept me going, that was it.

Adrenaline and me, Eona piped up. *Miracle two.*

And a miracle it was. Midnight had driven her sword into the same leg already wounded twice and Aaghar had fallen, no longer able to support himself, especially mid-kick. He roared in pain as she danced away, taking her sword and mine with her.

"Catch!" she called and tossed my sword at my feet. She looked rough, moving a bit slowly and awkwardly. I was fairly certain she'd taken one of his killer kicks and though I hadn't seen how it had hit her, she didn't have my toughness. I was surprised she was still alive.

I picked up my blade and moved in again as I caught movement from the corner of my eye. Turning, I saw Lyran back on his feet, though he was gasping awkwardly, not breathing well.

"He'll be weaker now that his dragon is dead," Lyran called.

Good to know.

Miracle three. Eona pushed the last of her strength within me.

Yet even just getting out those few words seemed to cost Lyran. His voice was strained and he coughed up blood.

The three of us slowly circled Aaghar. The dragon lord had drawn a long knife in his left hand. He couldn't move around, not well. He was on one knee and mostly stuck in place, still, none of us wanted to underestimate this formidable warrior.

"Still afraid of me?" Aaghar barked, clearly in pain. "You heard Lyran. I'm helpless, stuck, come on! Finish me!"

None of us would be goaded that easily.

Yet I knew I didn't have much longer before I succumbed to my injuries.

Lyran's eyes flicked to both of us, a signal. Attack as one and we might be able to finish this, and clearly Lyran was willing to take the brunt of Aaghar's attack as he was in front of the man.

He yelled and charged in.

I did the same, aiming for a spot I could see just below the lip of Aaghar's helm and above his gorget, a small opening, but...

Too much happened at once. Aaghar let Lyran hit him, the sword cutting into Aaghar's armor low on his side; catching there. At the same time, he hit Lyran, not with the knife, but with his wounded fist, which may be all that saved Lyran's life. Still Lyran was sent flying. The knife was sent stabbing back as Aaghar half spun. It clipped Midnight as she drove her sword down on Aaghar's shoulder. He cut a deep gash across her chest as she severed his arm.

I didn't hit my intended spot, Aaghar had shifted too much. Instead, my blade hit his gorget and deflected up, getting caught between his armor and helm. My sword was torn from my fingers. I dove away, seeing Aaghar's elbow headed for me, and came up in front of him.

Midnight was falling back, clutching her chest, which poured forth blood. Aaghar cried out at the loss of his arm — his good arm at that — but still didn't go down. Once again, rage filled his eyes. I was right there, in front of him, but had no weapon. With him on one knee, I could reach his face. So... I punched the exposed area, not covered by his helm. It barely did anything except, perhaps, rouse him from the shock of losing his arm.

He swung his bad arm at me, and I ducked it. I needed a weapon... and Lyran's sword was still stuck in Aaghar's side.

I dove again to that side of him, but even as I did, he rose on his good leg and spun his wounded leg at me in a feeble kick. I was only just able to duck under it.

Then I came up and grabbed the sword. I didn't even have to take it out, I yanked it to one side, shifting the blade inside of him, then surged myself upward as hard and fast as I could driving the blade up into his chest.

Aaghar screamed and collapsed. I fell as well, nearly limp now, my eyes starting to swell closed, but Aaghar was unmoving. He wheezed a long burbling breath... then was still.

I'd done it!

Miracle Four. Eona sounded exhausted.

But... Lyran and Midnight needed my healing ability.

Actually... so did I.

I used Ceph's manipulation to shift around my wounds. That took a lot out of me, and I was just a little too wounded to completely heal myself, but I was no longer in danger of my eye swelling closed or losing consciousness, except from fatigue.

I rose, first going to Aaghar and kicking that sword deeper into him. He didn't flinch. He was dead.

Stumbling over to Midnight, I knelt next to her where she lay. Her eyes were a little wild, her lips muttering words I couldn't understand. Her wound was far worse than I'd thought. Aaghar's blade had sliced across the bottom of one breast, then destroyed the other one. I could see her ribs. I put my hands upon her and began to heal her chest when I felt... her other wound. Aaghar's kick from earlier had hit her low on one side, crushing a few lower ribs and mangling her innards. She'd only been grazed, that's why she was still alive. Still, I couldn't heal it all, not as tired as I was.

So, I put a hand to the ground. It had worked for Eophon and me previously...

Drawing elements and energy from the earth itself

I sought to first replenish myself. Iron, for my blood, calcium for my bones, and finally — harder since it wasn't a metal — carbon to mend and strengthen the rest of me. I drew in a long breath and sighed it out. I felt better but was still so very weary. Then I went to work on Midnight, replacing her damaged areas with new elements from the earth.

She breathed a heavy sigh and shuddered, eyes closing. I knew she'd live, but she'd need lots of rest to fully recover. I couldn't afford to spend any more time on her, I had to see if Lyran was still alive!

I tried to rise, collapsing several times before my watery legs supported me. I stumble-walked over to where Lyran lay. I thanked the sun and moon that he was still breathing. That last, weaker-arm hit from Aaghar had torn away his jaw and crushed in the side of his face, but that was it. I fell next to him and touched him, feeling the wound on his face and his crushed chest from the first hit he'd taken. His ribs were shattered, and he had one collapsed lung. It was a wonder he'd been able to get up at all after that. But I had no energy left to heal him. And he'd die if I didn't do something.

Again, I pulled from the earth, mending the bones of his face and chest with calcium, Luckily, he had lots of other healthy areas to take from to mend his muscles and replenish him. It was my own fatigue which limited what I could do, but I made sure he'd live.

Miracle five. Eona's voice seemed distant as I collapsed into a dreamless sleep.

CHAPTER 23

DAWN

We fell to our knees, Swan and I, as we struggled physically and within our spirits, in a duel which would surely kill one of us.

Her first blast of energy had singed my side, the skin burned and painful. But I'd weakened her spirit-gift enough that she'd not been able to use her blast after that and her physical shields had gone down. Since then, we'd been fighting tooth and nail, resorting to our hands as we struggled for dominance.

Yet even as I tore through her spirit, she was winning the physical fight. She sat on top of me, hands clamped around my throat. I clawed my nails over her face, trying to get her to let up so I could get some needed air. Within her, she still resisted me and had somehow reached into my spirit as well. We exchanged blows both physical and spiritual, fighting for our very lives.

There were no words, no taunts, we were well past that. All energy was saved for the fight as we both grew weaker, beating upon each other.

But I had something she didn't. We were nearly even in power, both strong in spirit with a Lumani of great potency and vigor. Yet I was part Fey, beings far closer to the realm of spirit than humans, and that meant, in the realm of spirit I was stronger.

I could also control cloth and used that power now to tighten the collar of her blouse around her neck.

She kept one hand on the front of my neck, pressing down with all her weight, as her other came to my face. I felt it warm. She couldn't summon her beam of energy, but it seemed she had enough residual power to heat her hand. If she touched me, she'd burn my face.

I pulled back my fist and punched her hard in the jaw. Her head spun to the side, and she released me for just a moment, rolling off me. I gasped in air even as I rose on one arm and punched her again. She fell back. Now I was on top of her. Her arms flailed, useless, as I regained more of my breath.

I smiled. I'd won. I nearly had all her gift, and I was in control physically now.

No, wait, I feel something, Amya warned me.

"No!" Swan cried out, a long and drawn-out wail, eyes wide.

Her power... it's fading, but also building! Amya hissed, and I felt it too. Then Amya voiced our fears: *perhaps she has some ultimate revenge power, if she dies...*

...She'll take me with her.

But I couldn't stop, wouldn't stop. I ripped at her spirit and felt the last shreds of it pull away from her. *If I have to die to end this threat, I will,* I said to Amya. *When you're Bonded next, seek out my mother, tell her what happened.*

I will, Dawn. Amya was somber. He wouldn't try to reassure me now. We both knew this was the end. As the last of Swan's spirit was torn away, she began to glow.

Her desperate cry reached a new, ear-splitting pitch. Her head lolled back, eyes wild as she died, and she used one last drop of vengeance to punish the one killing her. Her spirit was mine, but with it came one last blast of energy.

Time seemed to slow.

The glow within her blossomed out and burned away her skin as a brilliant red light burst forth from her. I was consumed by it, my physical form burned away as well. Though it happened in an instant, I seemed to feel every agonizing moment of being incinerated.

I'd won. I'd killed her, taken her spirit, her gift, but

she'd had the last laugh it seemed and as the last of my body was consumed, I knew I too had died.

Blinding light.

Peace.

Yet...

I seemed to float over where we both had been, a massive charred mark upon the earth. Ashes fell softly around me... through me; all that remained of both of us.

And as I floated higher, I could see the entire field of battle. We had won the day, but the cost had been dire. Our forces were nearly wiped out. Aaghar and his dragon were dead, but our heroes were sorely wounded, having paid a heavy price for this victory; this impossible victory.

We had made the impossible possible...

But I had died and so many others had suffered, and I knew my death would cause even deeper wounds upon their souls.

I had no eyes, but still I wept bitter tears.

To be continued...

Don't miss the next book in the series!

Double Destiny
Shadows Over Elista: Book Five

They've won an impossible victory... but at what cost?

The dragon lord Aaghar is dead, his armies defeated, but the toll the battle took upon our heroes is devastating. Everyone is wounded and weary, and their little army of rebels is virtually wiped out.

But that isn't the worst of it... the only way for Dawn to defeat Swan was to sacrifice her own life.

Through the unbreakable link which ties Roo and Dawn together, Roo knows instantly that Dawn is dead... and yet, she can still sense a small part of her spirit. In a desperate attempt to save some vestige of her close companion, Roo does the unimaginable and bonds Dawn's soul to her own, bringing Dawn's essence to reside within her body before it fades forever.

Now the twin spirits are merged closer than ever. But what does this mean for the men who've dedicated their lives to these two women? How will this change the complicated dynamic of their relationship? Before these questions can be answered, news arrives that the remaining nine dragon lords, furious at the loss of their brother, are heading for Elista to wipe it out completely.

Now Roo and Dawn must find some way to come to terms with their twin souls in one body while preparing for a battle which, one way or another, will be their last.

OTHER BOOKS BY CLARA WILS

THE GRECIAN GODDESS TRILOGY

Kiss of the Goddess, book 1

Power of the Goddess, book 2

Bonds of the Goddess, book 3

THE MISTS OF ELISTA TRILOGY

Bonds and Blood, book 1

Shape and Shadows, book 2

Form and Fury, book 3

SHADOWS OVER ELISTA

Double Discover, book 1

Double Danger, book 2

Double Disaster, book 3

Double Doom, book 4

Double Destiny, book 5